Malady Manor

A Novel

Malady Manor is a novel. None of the characters existed and none of the events described in the book actually happened.

Malady Manor

By
Orrin Onken

SALISH PONDS PRESS LLC
FAIRVIEW, OREGON

To Dale

1

Things were out of hand. It was eight-thirty on Monday morning and I was working on my second Budweiser. I hadn't wanted to open the beer, or the one before it, and I didn't want the one I was sure to have after it. I put the can down on the coffee table and called Isol at work. It was a call I had wanted to make for months, but I hadn't had the strength to lift the phone until that morning. When Isol answered I said I wanted her to help me stop drinking. She was not surprised at the call. I had only recently discovered I was a drunk; she had known about it for a long time. When you single handedly keep Anheiser-Busch in business your wife notices. That night we talked about it together. We talked about my drinking, our commitment to each other, and our insurance coverage. We cried together. Talking about our insurance always made us cry.

The following morning I had a couple of Budweiers for breakfast and worked my way through the Yellow Pages looking for alcohol treatment programs. I learned that alcoholics were in reasonably high demand in Oregon. A drunk may not be of much use to most people, but in the medical world an insurance policy is a terrible thing to waste. For the first time in a long time the people I spoke to on the phone were happy to talk to me. Shopping for treatment made me feel wanted. The programs sold themselves, and I, the literally drunken judge, got to pick the winner.

I spent a lot of time looking at treatment alternatives. I talked with a waterfront detox center for the down and out that wanted me to get in a line at the front door before dawn and hope for an open bed. I talked with a couple of full service hospitals that promised not only to beat alcoholism but also be ready if I needed an emergency organ transplant. One place boasted an ocean view and a cure that consisted largely of golf and cable TV. I learned about in-patient programs, out-patient programs, aversion and diversion. This search took several days, filled several legal pads with notes, and required numerous cases of beer. After much deliberation and consultation with Isol, I chose the most expensive cure my insurance would cover.

The treatment center I picked had a real name but the patients never called it anything other than Malady Manor. The Yellow Pages ad for the Manor had a line drawing of the building that reminded me of *Wuthering Heights*. What the drawing didn't show was that the building stood in the center of Portland's industrial district. I didn't mind. I didn't pick the place because of the neighborhood. I picked it because it accepted my insurance and the receptionist had the sweetest phone voice of any facility in town.

One Thursday morning a well dressed woman from Malady Manor Inc. walked me through the facility and explained the basics of the Malady program. She spoke in hushed tones and exuded the earnest confidence that comes from working on commission. She explained that the program at the Manor was based upon the teachings of Alcoholics Anonymous. That meant nothing to me. I was concerned about architecture. If I was going to sober up I wanted an appropriately depressing place to do it. An abandoned convent in the middle of the Portland warehouse district seemed perfect. When we finished the tour, I disclosed the details of my insurance policy and promised to show up the following Monday with a suitcase and toothbrush.

I had enrolled in a twenty-one day residential treatment program: one day for each year of my drinking. Over the weekend I broke the news to my parents and my tavern buddies. My parents were supportive but suspicious. Each of my bar buddies pledged his support and silently thanked God it wasn't him. On Sunday I said farewell to the most constant companion I had ever had: alcohol. I spent a few melancholy final hours at the tavern, then went home to drink until the wee hours of the morning. In final tribute to my twenty-one year affair with booze I passed out that night with my glass half full.

On Monday I showed up at the Manor shortly before noon with five days worth of clean clothes, a few toiletries, and a stack of novels. My hangover from the previous night kept me company. I walked through the double doors of the Manor and was met inside by a bearded giant wearing work boots and overalls. He thrust an enormous hand at me and bellowed, "Hi. My name is John. I'm an alcoholic and a dope fiend."

I whimpered a hung-over "hello." The Goliath shook my sweaty hand and lumbered out the doors.

The sweet-voiced receptionist who had attracted me to the Manor in the first place turned out to be seventy-five years old if she was a day. She confiscated my luggage and ushered me into the accounting office where I disgorged more insurance information and pledged my first born in the event my insurance company declined to pay. Sobriety is free; treatment requires collateral.

After my visit to the accounting department they sat me down in a bare cubicle furnished with two chairs and a writing table. The time for my first drink of the day had long passed, and my hands were doing the sobriety shiver. A tall red-haired woman carrying a black binder came into the room and sat at the table across from me. The binder, my official entry in the bureaucracy of recovery, had my name, birthday, and social security number printed on the front.

The woman with the binder introduced herself as Joan, and for the next two hours I answered questions from Joan about my alcohol and drug use. The questions were oddly difficult to answer. At the tavern we reveled in war stories about drinking and drugging. Each tale was a Purple Heart in the war against sobriety, but in the little room at the Manor, being questioned in detail, the particulars escaped me. I remembered the places I lived and worked, but when it came to the drinking, all the days were the same. When I wasn't working I was loaded, when I did work I was hung over, and I hadn't worked in a long time. I gave her the most honest answers I could, and she wrote them down without comment. In having to tell it all to Joan, I realized that, despite the tavern war stories, my drinking had been boring. I was a run-of-the-mill alcoholic. I'd always hated the idea of average. Being an average drunk was the worst.

Once Joan was done writing in the binder, she showed me up to my room in the second floor dormitory. The ambiance in the dormitory was decidedly different from the floor below. The lobby area, where the public was allowed, held delicate Edwardian chairs and plush curved sofas. Mozart played through invisible speakers. The dorm area looked like a cross between a rent-by-the-week hotel and a bus station.

My room contained four beds and four writing desks—the desk drawers serving as a bureau for my clothes. My bed, piled with folded towels and sheets, stood next to a small window that had been sealed shut by the ivy growing up the outside of the building. At some point several decades before my arrival, plumbing had been inexpertly retrofitted into the building, leaving water and drain pipes visible along the high ceiling in the hall. The bathroom, three doors down, resembled the ones you find in the better minor league baseball stadiums.

Happy hour at the tavern was almost over by the time I'd put my clothes in the drawers of my writing desk, and I was definitely out of sync with the world. Joan located a healthy looking young man and introduced him as Robert. He was to be my roommate and my "buddy" for purposes of introducing me to the Manor routine. At the moment the only buddy I wanted came out of a beer tap, however, I put up with the kid long enough to get a tour of the dining room, laundry room and, thank God, the smoking room. After the tour I knew where to take each of my crucial bodily functions.

Before dinner they searched my belongings again. One of the apprentice jailers removed, unfolded, and examined everything I had with me. She sniffed my toothpaste, opened my bars of soap, and flipped through the pages of my books. Anything drug related or otherwise subversive had to go. I had been careful packing so everything except my nail clipper survived. The clipper, a potential weapon, was confiscated for my protection. No longer a danger to myself or others my buddy took me to the dining room.

Dinner started promptly at six o'clock in a room containing about twenty-five of my new colleagues. The diners were seated four to a table, waiting for those patients who had attained trustee status to deliver the food. I hadn't had a drink all day and abstinence was not being kind to me. The last thing I felt like was food. If forced to eat, I wanted a sullen meal among people who were at least as miserable as I was. The dinner companions I had were chatty, noisy, and annoying. I had expected a room full of alcoholics and drug addicts to look threatening and desperate. My colleagues were normal looking folks from different age groups and economic backgrounds. Some were a year or so short of graduating high school; others looked like retired schoolteachers. Most disturbing was that they were goofing around, laughing, and enjoying themselves. I had just turned my back on alcohol, the love of my life. Frivolity was an insult to my grief.

One of the Manor staff stood at his table and announced my name to the assemblage. The diners responded with an embarrassing round of applause, and I meekly waved to the crowd. I would learn later that this was the traditional welcome to new patients.

Toward the end of my drinking, food and I had grown apart. Eating was an annoyance that diluted the effect of alcohol and wasted good drinking time. My first meal at the Manor was a bland chicken casserole. I picked at it while my comrades gobbled. My stomach rebelled at the thought of swallowing any of the casserole, so I turned my attention to a vegetable soup served on the side. My hands were shaking badly enough by then that I was unable to consistently hit my mouth with the spoon.

After my awkward dinner we all retired to the smoking room. All addicts smoke. The smoking room was a messy smelly place with several beat-up couches and a coffee table. The ashtrays were overflowing and the curtains reeked of smoke. It felt like home.

Whether on the outside or in treatment, addicts make friends with each other quickly. In the smoking room I was promptly accepted into the fellowship of recovery. If you had a name and an addiction you were welcome. I had both, and within an hour the other patients were no longer strangers. I met Big John, the alcoholic and dope fiend, for the second time. I talked with, Frank, an alcoholic, Robert, my roommate the coke addict, and Rollo, another coke head. I met Patty the wino and Della the heroin addict. Everyone had a drug of choice, but most were crossovers and multi-users. Some were on leave from professions; some were on leave from jail, but in the smoking room, money, education, and social status meant nothing. All that mattered was that each of us had lost a good friend. My friend had been alcohol. For others it was cocaine or heroin. It didn't matter. We were all at the Manor to talk about our losses, and there is nothing an addict would rather do than talk about his addiction. If we couldn't defeat our addictions we'd talk them to death. We did most of the good talking in the smoking room.

Bedtime was at eleven o'clock. My hands were still shaking when I marked the first day off my little paper calendar. I climbed into bed and sweated between the sheets into the night.

The second day started at four o'clock in the morning when a young woman in medical garb walked into the room, flipped on the overhead lights, and proceeded to remove several gallons of blood from my right arm. To the medicos, there is nothing like a good bloodletting to give a person a jump-start on sobriety.

Detox is aggravated assault on the body, and food is the first line of attack. The seven thirty breakfast was huge and mandatory. My stomach, lined only for coffee and aspirin, went into caloric shock. Lunch was at noon sharp and, like everything else, mandatory. Dinner was at six and snacks were at nine-thirty. Everything was sugar free, caffeine free, and massive. The evening snacks alone could have sustained certain small countries for several weeks. Everyone ate. The alkies ate; the cokeheads ate; everyone ate. In the smoking room we talked our additions to death. In the dining room we buried them in carbohydrates.

When I wasn't eating I drank. All the alkies drank. We drank juice, milk, water, and anything else the

Manor cook could put in front of us. Dehydration from drinking alcohol had left us constantly thirsty. For the first few days I downed fruit juice so fast that I sloshed when I walked. All the new alkies sloshed. When two or more newbies walked down the hall together you could hear the sound of the ocean in the halls.

Food and healthy drink had an immediate effect. My urine changed from clear to a deep yellow. When I took a dump, I produced solid cylindrical turds rather than the odiferous soup I had been producing for years. The medical people took my blood pressure three times a day. All the new patients had their blood pressures taken, however, the staff was particularly careful with me. My shakes were persistent and dramatic. Alcoholism had elevated my blood pressure. One of the delightful side effects of detoxification was that when I stopped drinking it went up even higher. Withdrawal from alcohol can kill. Big John explained to me that in the severe cases, or in the event of chest pain, a patient gets lithium to control the rising blood pressure. He extolled the pleasures of lithium—instant serenity—and taught me how to fake the tremors that got you the pills. I declined his advice and made it through the day without.

During my third day at the Manor I received a full medical checkup. I was stripped, poked, prodded, and stabbed. I answered questions about my health, my father's health, my mother's health, and the general well-being of everyone I had ever known. The doctor said I was underweight, out of shape, and I smoked too much. My vision was bad, my reflexes were shot, my teeth were decayed, and my skin was rejecting my body. My heartbeat was too fast, my bowels were schizophrenic, and my liver was in open revolt. For a person with twenty years of drinking under my belt, I was in remarkably good shape.

The doctor assured me that all I had to do was completely change every aspect of my life and I would be fine. The trip to the doctor was precautionary. Detox was simply eating and waiting. I did both. The Manor staff seldom bothered me during the first few days, so I ate, smoked, and ate again. The coffee had no caffeine, the drinks no carbonation, but the food had calories. My shakes went away and my weight went up. I could think clearly in the morning. When the severest of my symptoms had retreated the staff suggested I tackle the disease.

During the first day or so at the Manor I had come into possession of a blue hardcover book entitled *Alcoholics Anonymous*. It was called the Big Book and everyone had one. The Manor staff was constantly referring to it, quoting from it, and encouraging people to read it. At first this put me off, but one day, against my better judgment, I picked it up and started to read. It had big print and easy words. The style was *The Grapes of Wrath* written by a committee, and the message chilled me to the bone. The book and the people at the Manor were suggesting that I stop drinking forever. The concept of lifelong abstinence was simply beyond me. I could accept detox as annoying but necessary respite for body and soul on the way to learning to drink normally, but total abstinence seemed like cutting off my legs to get handicapped parking. The message in the Big Book so disturbed me that I put it away and went to the smoking room to incinerate a pack of cigarettes.

2

I think I was born alcoholic. All I needed was one good drunk to prove it. That drunk occurred after my junior year in high school. Partying with friends, I drank malt liquor until I passed out on the floor. When it was time for me to leave, my pals rousted me from unconsciousness and poured me into my car. On the way home, amid other traffic blunders, I stopped in front of a red motel sign and waited patiently for it to turn green. In the morning I was the one who turned green. I vomited most of the day. My head throbbed. The hangover lingered for three days, but before the hangover was half over, I wanted to do it again.

Liquor was always my drug of choice, but until I turned twenty-one, liquor was difficult to obtain in the quantities I needed. At the high school I attended marijuana was easier to get, more compact, and generally less messy. I smoked a lot of it, but it never became my love. My love was beer—cases and cases of beer.

I didn't drink often in high school. If I possessed liquor, which was seldom, I saved it for the weekends. But when I drank I drank to get drunk. I didn't drink to overcome shyness, be part of a gang, or to be sociable. I drank to feel the effect of alcohol, and the more I drank the more I liked it. From the very beginning, I had no use for one or two drinks. I drank to get stumbling down drunk.

When I left home to attend college alcohol became more available, but drinking was not the fashion. Protests against the Vietnam War were in full swing.

The fashionable users smoked pot and dabbled in hallucinogens. I did lots of both, but if left alone, my drug of choice came in a bottle.

I graduated from college and set off to see the country, reform the world, and write the great American novel. Shortly thereafter I was living in San Francisco and embracing bohemianism while I worked at a chain bookstore in a strip mall. When I wasn't working I was writing. While I wrote, I drank. Drinking didn't help me write, but if I drank enough I didn't have to write. In my alcohol fantasies I was already famous. Alcohol made me a genius.

After five years in San Francisco I decided I wanted to own a car. In order to buy a car I needed a real career. To get a career I sold all my books and did what everyone else did in the seventies—I signed up for law school.

My drinking had changed while I was in San Francisco. I still loved to get drunk. I still separated my drunks by days or even weeks. But I'd also begun to need a certain amount of alcohol every day to feel normal. I'd buy a six pack after work every day and it would be gone before I went to bed. It didn't get me drunk. It made me feel comfortable, and it relaxed me enough to sleep.

Law school made it easy to drink. I could schedule my classes late in the day. I could skip them all together. The studies didn't allow me a lot of opportunities to really tie one on, so I upped my daily drinking to compensate. By my third year I was drinking half a case of Budweiser every day.

While getting my law degree I had an odd sort of arrogance about my drinking. I was near the top of my class and was chosen to be editor-in-chief of the law review. Alcohol makes a person insane, but it doesn't make him stupid. I took a perverse pride in the fact that I could outperform a hundred other law students and still down a half case of brew every night. I had to keep this accomplishment to myself though. The drinking was secret—so secret that I wouldn't return my beer cans for the deposit out of fear the clerks would know how much I drank. I wouldn't throw them in the trash for fear that the garbage man might count them. For over a year I threw the cans into the unfinished attic of my apartment via a trap door in the ceiling of one of the closets—a present for some future occupant.

I graduated from law school with low-level academic honors and passed the bar exam. During my legal studies I had acquired the car I'd wanted, but my desire for that respectable career had diminished significantly as a result of contact with real lawyers. I had to do something, however, because law school had left me in serious debt. That debt was motivation to work.

I joined a respected Oregon firm where the lawyers had the manners of gentlemen and the morals of jackals. I lacked both the manners and the morals to fit in, so I got even with them by drinking. I quickly learned that there are not enough hours in a day to work full time and drink too. Practicing law can't be scheduled to start late and end early. Forty hours a week cut my drinking time to the bone, and the big shots at the firm hinted that new associates should pay their dues at the rate of fifty to sixty hours a week. They put me under so much pressure to produce legal work that for a while I even tried to cut back on my alcohol consumption. It didn't work, but I tried.

While at the firm I burdened myself with a house, another car, two purebred dogs, and a rack of silk ties. I made the payments on the things I bought and still had money in my pocket. I'd never been so rich in my life. I was respected, respectable, and supremely miserable. Most people, I think, buy things in order to feel good and to enhance their quality of life. I bought things in a desperate attempt to look normal.

For many good reasons, the big firm and I didn't work out. I left it to team up with an older lawyer who practiced by himself in the suburbs. He was an eccentric who was tolerated, but not well-liked, by other lawyers. He had a knack for making money and a great work ethic, but was handicapped by the fact that he didn't understand law. He got it wrong every time. I was a perfect partner for him. I didn't get much work done, but I had an intuitive grasp of law. I knew what would work for a client and how to do it. Together, the two of us made one decent attorney.

The suburban practice accommodated my drinking. My boss seldom bothered me about production so I had an hour or so a day to close my office door and sleep away some of the hangover I brought to work every morning. Because I understood law I took over the court appearances and trial work. Trials start late and end early.

For a while everything clicked. My boss brought in the cases and could usually, through abrasive persistence, negotiate a resolution that paid the office expenses and my salary. If he could not, I took the case to court.

About this time I took up a new hobby: tavern drinking. In the taverns I learned that I was not alone in my love of alcohol. The tavern became my first stop after leaving work where a couple of pints took the edge off. I could then go home, change clothes, walk the dogs and eat my one meal of the day. Fortified by food, exercise, and a few more beers, I would go back to the tavern again and drink until I could sleep.

The tavern gave me a social life. I had friends, golfing buddies, and soon enough, a lover. In the taverns I didn't have to hide my drinking. Drinking was a badge of honor—a ticket to the good life.

The good life, however, was coming to an end. My boss went into semi-retirement and turned the business over to me. I no longer had a salary. Paying rent, figuring taxes, and generating business became my responsibility. I was worse than bad at it; I simply could not do it.

3

At Malady Manor everything happened at the sound of the bell. The bell was one of those hand held affairs used by Salvation Army Santas. Every week one unlucky inmate was appointed bell ringer. Five minutes before each event of the day the bell ringer walked up and down the dormitory halls summoning us to our appointed tasks. For the first couple of days, while detoxing, the bell was convenient. I didn't wear a watch and seldom knew where I was supposed to go next. I could wait for the bell and follow the crowd. The bell annoyed a lot of people, but I liked it.

They kept me isolated from the outside world for the first five days. I couldn't use the phone, receive mail, or have visitors. They forced food down my throat three times a day until I started to enjoy eating again. Exercise was mandatory, and everyone was assigned physical exercise according to his or her abilities. My assignment was volleyball for an hour every afternoon. We took to the court—alkies on one side, addicts on the other—with Big John, the alkie-dope fiend officiating at the net. People walking by the Manor grounds could hear Big John's booming voice: "Seven, ten, addicts." We made noise, cheated, and traded insults. "How many addicts does it take to change a light bulb?" "Two, one to stick in the bulb and one to tie off the socket." My reflexes improved, my muscles ached, and I started to sleep through the night.

The volleyball, like everything else, began and ended on time. Our schedule was sacred and unalterable. A golf pro practices his swing over and over to develop muscle memory that will last him through the stress and distractions of the tournament. At the Manor we were developing muscle memory for living sober.

Counselor's assistants woke us at six-thirty. We made beds and took medications before breakfast. After breakfast we met to hear a spiritual reading, listen to announcements, and collectively agree that we were going to do exactly the same thing today that we did yesterday. We euphemistically called this gathering "meditation."

After meditation we moved to the dining room to hear the counselors lecture on drug or health related subjects. The lectures resembled the health classes I'd taken in high school, the difference being that as adults we were allowed to swear in class.

After lecture we met for group. Group was an event in which we gathered six or eight to a room under the guidance of a counselor to reveal and discuss the sordid details of our remarkably dull lives. Group was the longest and most difficult segment of the day.

After lunch we would sleep through an educational videotape or two about addiction and related diseases. After the video we had exercise, and after exercise we met to read aloud about the twelve steps of Alcoholics Anonymous. Then there was medication again and the evening meal. Dinner was followed by a speaker, or a mock AA meeting in which we pretended to be real alcoholics living in the free world. All of the activities started on time and ended on time. We didn't skip a meeting or knock off early. We didn't call in sick or take a long lunch. With some prodding from the staff, we did it when we were in the mood and when we weren't in the mood. After the first few days, I could go through the motions by muscle memory alone. Like the golfer swinging his club, I went from one room to the next without having to think. Fed, exercised, and hypnotized, I did treatment.

The work at the Manor was shared among administration, counselors, counselor's assistants, and housekeeping. Fortunately for the patients, these organizational layers seldom communicated with each other. In addition, we had a minister, a doctor, and a couple of itinerant psychologists. Everyone at the Manor, from the big boss to the lowliest cook, was a recovering something or other.

Administration consisted of supervisors, admission officers, accountants, and secretaries. These people remained anonymous. They hung around offices near the front door, drank caffeinated coffee from personalized cups, and did their best to avoid any direct contact with patients. Although seldom seen, administration struck terror into the other levels of the organization. The mere mention of administration caused the other tiers of staff to become furtive and suspicious. By trickle down, the patients came to fear administration as well. Woe be it to the poor patient who was unlucky enough to get a counselor's assistant in trouble with administration. When walking through the administrative area near the front doors, the patients bowed their heads in respect and avoided eye contact with anyone they met. Better safe than sorry.

Just below administration were the counselors. These people had offices close to the patient rooms in the dormitory. Counselors had college degrees. The men wore ties and the women wore dresses. Every patient was assigned his or her personal counselor, and each counselor kept voluminous records on his or her patients. Behind closed office doors the counselors met one-on-one with patients and designed the program of treatment that would be most distasteful to that particular person. Like a high school teacher, the counselors handed out homework, graded it, and made us present it to the class in group.

Assistant counselors or C.A.'s did the day to day patient herding. They ousted us from bed in the morning and stuck us between the sheets at night. They handed out medicine and confiscated contraband. They were our everyday jailers and controlled all the little things that make life livable. The C.A.'s were generally only a few months out of detox centers themselves. Thus, they were immune to the lies, schemes, and cons we alkies had come to rely upon to get by in the world. They were petty, spiteful, and self-centered. They were our kind of people.

Our C.A.s had not survived addiction and recovery without developing a few personality quirks. On graveyard shift we had Aaron, the sleeping giant. He was the reason Malady Manor could advertise twenty-four hour care. This huge man slept all night at a desk in the dormitory hall. No one ever saw him come or go, and no one ever saw him awake. Another C.A., Pixie

Patty had survived heroin addiction to live a life stranded in a high school revival of *Peter Pan*. She worked afternoons, tripping fantastic through the halls spreading smiles and fairy dust. On swing shift we suffered through cowboy Bob. He was an alkie who stood five foot two in his cowboy boots. He had memorized the Manor rule book and was willing to recite sections aloud at purely random times during the day. He was assigned the job of meal monitor where he was forever threatening to ban someone from the dining room for peeking inside the covered serving dishes before the signal to eat.

The remainder of the Manor staff worked on the edges of treatment. The cooks kept us fed but were seldom seen. The maintenance people kept the place clean and stayed away from the patients. There was a doctor who was always on vacation. His geriatric nurse wrote down the patients' medical complaints in a book and made sure the book was always kept in the same place in case the doctor should return from vacation and need to look at it. The Manor had two psychologists who spoke only to the counselors and to administration. One of them was an older woman who was writing a paper on excessive flossing. Her research kept her at the dental school across town most of the time. The other psychologist was a younger woman with a stutter and a wandering eye.

The staff was rounded out by Sky Pilot, the pastor. No one ever used his real name. Sky Pilot had to tend to our religious needs and take us through step five of the twelve steps. Within the first couple of days of arrival at the Manor each patient was sent to Sky Pilot for religious consultation.

The patients were not generally religious. Most of them hadn't thought about God in years. A few hated God, and a couple of them thought they were God. Sky Pilot listened to them one and all, and everyone felt sorry for him. When Sky Pilot wasn't helping others to enlightenment he spent his time wallowing in guilt over the fact that he'd never been addicted to anything and that he'd married a woman half his age. Every new patient offered to help him with the first dilemma. No one understood the second. Some people just need to feel guilty.

The various levels of staff shared the job of imposing order at the Manor. It was a difficult and thankless task. They had to drag the cokeheads out of bed, get the alcoholics into bed, keep the pill heads out of the medication room, and enforce an endless list of rules and regulations.

"No coffee outside the dining room." "No food in the dorm area." "No smoking during exercise." "No phone calls before five." "No TV after eleven." "No feet on chairs." "No sleeping during lecture." "No being late." "No leaving early." "Make your beds." "Take your meds." "Clear your table." "Empty your ash trays." "Sign out." "Sign in." "Be quiet." "Speak up." "Sit." "Stand." "Read." "Listen." "Think."

In order to remind us of the importance of precise routine we had Saturday rules meetings. These meetings emphasized the fact that we did not live in anything resembling a democracy. Each of the Manor rules was read aloud by a patient. One of the staff then explained that all rules were to be interpreted in the most annoyingly restrictive way possible, and any rule which seemed to leave a patient latitude for choice only appeared that way because of typographical errors.

In addition to the written rules, the patients were expected to obey the unwritten rules as well. The basic unwritten rule was that anything not specifically permitted was prohibited. The other unwritten rules clarified the basic rule. We learned that deodorant was mandatory but foot spray was a danger to our continued sobriety. We were admonished that fire exits were not to be used during fire drills but could be used during real fires. We learned that in case of a dispute about the rules there was an unwritten grievance procedure that required that all grievances be in writing. It was against the rules however, to say anything else about the grievance procedures. The rules meetings tended to be short.

All of us hated the rules. Rebelliousness was everywhere. No one had any deep objection to a set routine. Prior to coming to the Manor my drinking routine had been as uniform and regular as boot camp. The time, the tavern, and the table were the same every day. I had one way to drink in the morning, one way to drink in the afternoon, and another way to drink at night. The habits of addicts and alkies are more precise than those of normal people. The problem with the rules at the Manor was that they were not our rules, and that we didn't like.

Nobody likes to be told what to do, but being

alcoholic, I took it particularly hard. Self-determination was the cornerstone of my drinking existence. I viewed life as a series of choices; an exercise in judgment and will. Choices were my birthright, and I wasn't about to give them away. Like many people who would rather be right than happy, I was perfectly willing to choose misery to assure myself I was still in charge. When told to wake up, I tried to sleep. When told to sit, I stood. When told to be on time, I was late. I wasn't trying to improve life at the Manor or lead people to a better way. I was assuring myself that I still controlled my own behavior. Only when I felt in control of my own life could I get any real pleasure out of telling other people how they should run theirs. An alcoholic does not need to be drunk to know how the world should run. He is simply louder about it after a few drinks.

4

During the first few days of 1990 I walked away from law and into the abyss of serious addiction. Everything I had collected from six years of practicing fit into an apple box. It took less space in the storage room than my golf clubs.

Isol and I both bought into the idea that I just needed a hiatus from the craziness of the courtroom. The word "burnout" was popular at the time. We collaborated on the theory that I was a victim of professional burnout. Besides, I hadn't had a true vacation since I first started to practice. All I needed was a little time and a little healing.

I quit paying my malpractice insurance. I let my bar membership lapse. I stopped paying all my debts and collected my assets. For reasons I didn't really understand, I set in for a long siege. Little did I know the enemy was inside.

In order to hide my addiction, I had always kept an impenetrable wall around my personal life. My work life and home life never mixed. My coworkers never came to where I lived. My wife never went to my office. Once I no longer had work to go to, I reinforced the wall around my home. Everyone I knew from work and law school was cut off. Many of my clients and coworkers had considered me a friend, but when their phone calls to my home went unanswered, they stopped calling.

My creditors, however, did not hesitate to call. Within a few months I could tell a collection agent by the way the phone rang. When the collection agents didn't get paid the lawsuits started. The same process server I had often hired to serve others was serving me summonses at my home.

I didn't mind being sued. I had sued so many people in my life that I considered it a case of what goes around comes around. What assets I did have I had placed out of reach of creditors. Money had never been more than a game to me. Some times you have it; sometimes you don't. I was prepared to go without.

I kept the lawsuits that had been filed against me in a blue binder. Some of them were attempts to collect money I owed. Others were malpractice claims. When the binder was full, I took them all down to the bankruptcy court and sent my creditors packing. Some of the people I owed money did not take kindly to this. I endured a fair amount of bankruptcy litigation to make it all go away, but, in the end the rulings all went my way. I knew the law. Suing me was a waste of time.

The bankruptcy litigation wound down. I was starting the new decade with no debts, no credit, and no job. I had income from unemployment based upon a stress claim and settled in for a pleasant and idle autumn.

I played golf, I went camping with friends, and I drank. During the week, while Isol worked, I dabbled at looking for a job. Now and again I dropped in at the law library to read a little law. I explored the city. I explored the taverns.

My watering hole was Taps Tavern, just two blocks from the apartment. Taps became an extension of my

living room. The owner of Taps catered to the genera-
tion reared on television, marijuana, and the Grateful
Dead. At Taps the beer flowed, the music played, and
the pool tables were always busy. Taps was my social
life. I held an honored place in a group known to itself
and others as the Lemmings. The Lemmings were as
much a part of Taps as the furniture. We were about
ten men and women who shared, cared, and dared to
drink beer. We drank together, we played golf together,
and we reassured each other that as long as we stayed
together all would be right with the world. I met Isol
while drinking with the Lemmings. They were the
people I allowed in my home.

The Lemmings consisted of a couple of salesmen, a
couple of machinists, a printer, a court clerk, and a
variety of students, troubadours, and wannabes. We
met at least once a day at Taps. Golf trips started at
Taps and ended at Taps. Workdays were forgotten at
Taps. Meeting the Lemmings after a day in the office
had always been the best part of my working day. With
no office to go to, it was the only part of my day.

That fall Isol and I spent a lot of time in the forests
around Portland. During her vacations and over long
weekends we loaded our truck and headed to an
isolated camping spot on the slopes of Mount Hood.
Isol would fish and smoke pot. I painted bad watercolor
landscapes and drank.

When the fall rains came and Isol's vacation days
were gone, we settled even deeper into a routine of
drugs and alcohol. I took her to work in the morning
then returned to our apartment to sleep off the rest of

the previous days drinking. If I woke early enough and had the energy, I went to the unemployment office or the law library. Occasionally, I had a job interview, but even if the employers couldn't spot the alcoholism, a bankrupt ex-lawyer is a very dangerous person to hire. No one wanted to take the chance, and I didn't much like the idea of working anyway.

By mid-afternoon I would be at Taps to quaff a couple of beers and do the crossword puzzle in the daily paper. The barkeeps would draw my beer as I came through the door so it would be ready by the time I reached the bar. I would wander home about four o'clock to straighten up the apartment and catch Oprah. I'd pick up Isol from work shortly after five. She would change clothes in the truck and smoke some marijuana on the way to Taps.

I had drawn a group caricature of the Lemmings. The drawing hung on the wall at Taps. The picture was entitled *The Lost Supper,* after all the meals we had missed there. Beneath the picture we talked and told jokes. We laughed. We argued politics, religion, and the mysteries of the universe.

We referred to marijuana as "church" because the Lemmings always smoked it behind a church across the street from Taps. If someone had church, and someone usually did, the Lemmings would take leave from the table and adjourn to the alley behind the real church to smoke. Isol was particularly fond of church. I liked the beer better. Once services were over we all reappeared at the table, reclaiming our half-consumed beers. And so it went every evening.

After Taps, Isol and I would drive to the store to pick up a half case and some dinner. We'd cook, and I'd eat my only meal of the day. After dinner I bathed while Isol made up a nest of pillows and blankets in front of the television. A couple of hits of Oregon's finest green bud settled us in for the evening. Isol would fall asleep and I'd polish off the half case.

We did our serious drinking on Friday night. We looked forward to Friday all week long. The pressure of her work and the guilt of my idleness were released on Fridays. I would stock the refrigerator early to reduce our chances of a drunk driving arrest. I'd start drinking about noon to prepare for the evening. Isol would get off work at five. We'd make a quick stop at the apartment for some church and a change of clothes. By five thirty we would be settled into Taps for the night. On Fridays, all the Lemmings would be there and everyone in the tavern would be an apprentice Lemming, honorary Lemming, or the ex-wife of a Lemming. It was not at all uncommon for Isol and I to know every customer at Taps. The challenge list at the pool table filled the chalkboard. The pinball machines were crowded and the rock and roll was turned up loud.

We drank beer, we went to church, and we drank more beer. We shot pool, talked, and drank more beer. Isol tried to match me drink for drink, but I had years more experience and substantially more body weight. If she started to fade she might convince me to go home for something to eat, or at least have a chiliburger at Taps. Whether eating or not, we kept the beer glasses full.

By midnight most of the Lemmings would have wandered away. Isol and I staggered to our pickup truck and forced our eyes to focus long enough to drive the two blocks home.

Once back in the apartment Isol would have a Budwieser and pass out on the living room floor. I liked that. It allowed me a little quiet time to drink, think, and watch late night movies. I'd work on the half case I'd gotten earlier. All alone I could float peacefully on a sea of alcohol dreams.

On these Friday nights all was right with the world. All the people who'd harmed me, those who had forced me out of law or turned me down for jobs, had gotten their comeuppance. I was back on top. I relived the trials I'd won in court years ago feeling more glory from my drunken memory than I had from the real thing. I would stay in the reveries until my eyes no longer focused on the television. When I couldn't see anymore, I'd stumble into bed. Isol would wake up on the living room floor sometime in early morning, shivering from the cold, and join me beneath the covers.

Saturday morning the apartment would be littered with Budweiser cans. Many were half full because in my late night drinking if I set a can down I would often be unable to find it again. I'd get a new one and sip it until I finished it or lost it as well. Isol would take the edge off the morning hangover with a couple hits of church. I'd have a beer.

The Christmas season arrived and our finances were stretched to the maximum. Isol's salary and my unemployment brought in barely enough to cover our bills and our drinking. There was nothing to spare for much in the way of Christmas. As adults often do in lean times, we decided to forgo gifts for each other. We decorated a tree, gave small presents to relatives, and went to the liquor store for some special Christmas libation. Isol did most of the work. I wasn't a Christmas person.

On Christmas eve we partied with the Lemmings at Taps for most of the afternoon and then went home to watch a video and drink away the rest of the evening. Isol had decorated the apartment. The evening was festive and the vodka was Russian.

On Christmas morning there were several gaily wrapped presents under the tree. Isol had given me several things: personal things and fun things. I opened the presents from her and when I finished with mine there were none left under the tree. I'd gotten nothing for her.

I went into the kitchen to start breakfast. When I came back into the living room, Isol was crying. I put my hand on her shoulder to comfort her. Through her sobs she told me, "A pair of socks. All I wanted from you was a pair of socks."

5

My buddy Robert, the young man who showed me around Malady Manor on my first day, was also my roommate. He was in for cocaine and alcohol; a combination I'd rather liked myself. A year or so before coming to the Manor he had received an insurance settlement of over $100,000 from a car accident. He proceeded to put enough cocaine up his nose and into his arms to be flat broke within nine months. Robert didn't trust anyone at the Manor, and the other patients distrusted him. I doubt he trusted me either, but he liked me and enjoyed asking me legal questions. One day, he confided in me that he was only going through the motions at the Manor because his father had pressured him into it. He didn't really have a drug problem and had nothing in common with the rest of us.

I had two other roommates in an adjoining dorm room. One was a male nurse named Andy, and the other was an alcoholic Indian called Jack. Andy was a friendly gay man who had abused nearly every drug a person might find in a hospital pharmacy. Jack was silent and withdrawn. He'd been brought in by people from the reservation during my third night at the Manor and left there without soap, money, or a change of clothes. The tribe was paying his bill for treatment but hadn't put out for toiletries. Jack spent of lot of time mumbling to his Indian ancestors.

The spiritual father of the patients was Big John, the behemoth Santa Claus who had met me at the door on the first day. John had lived the other American dream. He got high in the fifties while riding the rails when, according to him, you could still buy the good stuff at any corner drug store. He had a Purple Heart and a missing finger from the Korean War as a result of shooting heroin into an artery instead of a vein. He'd made pruno, a prison wine made from kitchen scraps, while doing a fifteen year prison term for manslaughter. In his golden years he'd settled down to simple alcoholism, militant unionism, and a featherbed job at the shipyards. When sober he was a regular at Morning Glory, an early morning AA meeting held in an old tin building near the docks where they did fire and brimstone AA.

Big John did everything full tilt. When he drank he drank day and night until his unemployment checks ended and the union was out of patience. He claimed that the first time he got sober three different taverns went out of business. When sober, he proclaimed the gospel of sobriety like a preacher at a revival meeting.

Big John was impossible to dislike. His never-ending tales of addiction, despair, and redemption all ended with the hand of the Lord pulling him from the murky waters. But a twinkle in his eye belied his many conversions. The adventures he described on the way to the abyss were always more colorful than the sobriety to which redemption brought him. Theoretically, he told his stories to dissuade others from making the same mistakes. However, everyone suspected that given the chance he'd do every bit of it over again.

The natural question, the one everyone always

asked, was "Why? Why, if you stayed sober so long did you start drinking again?" Big John loved the question, and, I believe, hoped to get asked. He'd smile broadly and proclaim, "Why? Because I'm an alcoholic, that's why. That's what alcoholics do. We are powerless over alcohol."

Big John's stories in the smoking lounge started the ball rolling for the rest of us and the tall tales of drinking and drugging came tumbling out. The quirks of our addictions, deep secrets in the normal world, became the currency of conversation and humor. Drinking and drugging does have its moments. If it didn't there wouldn't be millions of people in bars every Saturday night.

Some of the staff felt that Big John's jocularity showed a lack of commitment to sobriety and that his periodic treatment stays trivialized the recovery process. I had doubts whether Big John would die a sober man, but Big John's stories reminded me that there had been some good times. I didn't have to give up my memories of the good times in order to acknowledge the bad ones. Big John had regrets, but no remorse, and drunk or sober he seemed to love being alive. That was something I wanted.

On my fifth day at the Manor, after lunch, I took tests. I took intelligence tests, personality tests, logic tests, language tests, aptitude tests and a *let's-see-how-crazy he-really-is test*. Most of the tests took only a few minutes and were carefully timed by a C.A. The last one, however, was as thick as a phone book and filled with questions like, was I secretly controlled by aliens, or, would I rather be a weatherman or a panda bear. The C.A. administering this monstrosity told us that the test should take three hours to complete, but if anyone finished early, he or she could have smoke time until the dinner bell. I whipped through the thing in an hour.

After the test I hurried to the smoking room and lit up. The room had once been a sunroom for the old ladies who lived there when the Manor had been a retirement home. That day the big windows were open so the spring air could clean out the smell of old cigarettes. The trees on the Manor grounds were in bloom. I sat in a ray of sun and stared out the window. The blooming foliage and big pines hid the industrial area that surrounded the Manor. I felt safe, warm, and comfortable. I noticed the feeling. I was having a genuine and pleasant reaction to the world around me. Then I noticed myself starting to notice things.

Jack, my Indian roommate, shuffled into the room and stood at the far end.

"Hi, Jack," I said. He didn't respond. That wasn't unusual for him. "How are you feeling?"

"I broke my ribs," he said. "They hurt when I walk."

"How did it happen?"

"Some men beat me up . . . I fell down."

I decided to change the subject. "What's your drug of choice, Jack?" I pretended not to have assumed he was alcoholic solely because he was Indian.

"My fiancé died on December 14, 1989. We were going to be married."

"I'm sorry," I said.

"I was driving," he continued. "Sometimes, after that, I drank whiskey. I would drink for a month, one month, and then I wouldn't drink. I could stop for a year and then drink for one month."

"Do you need anything?" I asked him. The patients had chipped in to provide Jack with a few toiletries and a couple pair of clean socks.

"No brothers here, just white people," he said. "I can't do what they want here because of my ribs. White men beat me up."

"Do you live on the reservation?" I asked, hoping to avoid the racial issue.

"I disgraced my people," he said.

The conversation was not getting better. Fortunately, Pixie Patty arrived to herd Jack back to watchng a video about anger control. "Jack," she admonished, "you can't just wander off in the middle of the tape." She took him by the arm like a nurse moving a geriatric patient. Jack looked at the floor and shuffled toward the door with Patty. On her way out Patty eyed me suspiciously.

"I'm excused. I finished the test early," I told her. She accepted my explanation and went back to tending Jack. That was the longest conversation I ever had with Jack.

The day of the tests and my conversation with Jack was also my last day of isolation. I got phone privileges that evening and was on the list of people allowed Sunday visitors. The pay phone hung on the wall at one end of the dormitory next a blackboard with the hours from 5:00 P.M. to 11:00 P.M. marked off in ten-minute segments. Beneath the phone was a chair to sit in while you talked. I signed up for 5:20 that evening.

I met Stevie for the first time while putting my name on the blackboard. Pixie Patty and one of the counselors were escorting her down the hallway. The counselor was carrying her luggage while Patty directed Stevie toward a one-person dorm room in the women's section.

"Get your fucking hands off me," Stevie yelled at Patty. Swearing at the staff was forbidden. I sat down in the phone chair to watch. When the three of them were directly in front of me, Stevie pulled loose from Patty's grip. Leaning over so that her face was six inches from my own, she spat the words, "Fuck you," into my face. I knew right then that Stevie and I were destined to become friends.

The three of them disappeared into the empty single room, and I went back to the smoking room. I'd been there about twenty minutes when Stevie stormed in. She clawed at her pack of cigarettes, throwing the torn cellophane on the floor. "I'm gonna kick the shit out of that bitch," she declared. She sat down and lit her cigarette with shaking hands. "What are you in for?" she asked, blowing a thick stream of smoke into the room. She didn't seem to remember me from the conversation by the phone.

"Booze," I said. "How about you?"

"My god damn pervert of a doctor—H.M.O. homo—the cocksucker. My fuckin' husband threw me out. He doesn't know who he's fucking with. Is this the only place you can smoke around here? That Patty bitch is going to get her ass kicked."

Stevie had race brain. Her thoughts were running in circles. Past, present, and future were mixed together.

"What's your drug of choice?" I asked. She snuffed out her half-finished cigarette and started another.

"Pain pills. Percodan, seconal. The whole fucking pharmacy. My goddamn doctor did it. I should have cut his balls off when I had the chance."

Cowboy Bob came in and told Stevie she had to go down to accounting. "Fuck you, perv," she responded.

I didn't see Stevie again for three days. She lasted a few hours in her room and was taken to the infirmary where she could cuddle up to the barf bucket. Withdrawal from alcohol is potentially fatal, but withdrawal from pills is the ugliest.

Stevie sparked a lot of gossip among the patients. She was a real estate agent from a relatively affluent suburb west of Portland. She had two kids and her husband had once been a member of a motorcycle gang. She was the kind of person who made an impact on others, even when she was absent. We had seen her in the grip of withdrawal and were curious who she would turn out to be when sober.

That evening I called home. I hadn't talked to Isol since I had arrived. The conversation was strained and tentative. Both of us were afraid. She had stopped going to Taps the day I entered the Manor. A couple of the Lemmings had been bringing her meals at the apartment so she wouldn't have to eat alone. Nevertheless, she was lonely. Our marriage had been built around drugs. We could only hope it would still be there if we weren't using. I filled her in about what had happened to me, the people I'd met, and the routine at the Manor. We didn't ask big questions.

After dinner that night there was no speaker so we gathered in the dining room for a mock AA meeting. Daniel, one of the patients, volunteered to act as chairman. We all took seats and prepared to act like real recovering alcoholics and addicts.

The patients segregated themselves by age. The young males sat together as far away from the chairman as possible, looking like teenaged hoods avoiding the attention of the teacher. Those that could be loosely termed middle aged sat toward the front. The older patients sat on the edge so as to be noticeable only in the peripheral vision of the chairman. There were about twenty-five of us in all.

Daniel announced that the topic of the meeting would be our personal conceptions of a supreme being. This was Daniel's favorite subject and he talked about it no matter where he was or what other people were talking about. His choice brought a round of whispered boos from the back of the room. Frank, one of the senior citizens, announced that he never attended an AA meeting that had a topic and he wasn't going to participate. Melissa yelled that no one was supposed to be talking until we read the Twelve Traditions. Someone else told her to shut up because everyone had already heard the Twelve Traditions in step study. Daniel then got Frank to read the Twelve Traditions because his part would then be over and the rest of us could continue with the topic. Eventually, Daniel talked for a while about his conception of God and how it related to Taoism and the philosophy of Bubba Free John. During this monologue the rest of the patients broke up into discussion groups about whatever subject happened to come up. When Daniel finished talking and managed to quiet everyone, he asked a volunteer to share. Other than Frank, who volunteered that Daniel was so full of shit that he couldn't see straight, no one wanted to talk. Melissa finally said that she was a Methodist, that her parents were Methodists, and no one was going to convince her there was anything wrong with being a Methodist.

Outside of the Manor alcoholics meet at AA meetings to share their experiences while drinking and in recovery. At the Manor we gathered to bicker among ourselves and blame each other for making a mockery of our mock meeting. In AA people share their struggles with addiction by telling about their lives. At the Manor we shared our frustrations with sobriety by telling each other what to do. Toward the end of the hour, one of the patients raised his hand, and when called upon, suggested that we adjourn the mock meeting and reconvene as a kangaroo court.

After the meeting we went upstairs to smoke and laugh it all off. An hour passed and most of the smoking room crowd wandered off to the television room or to evening snacks. Daniel, Big John, and I remained.

Daniel was our envoy to the universe. Left over from the Age of Aquarius, he had settled down to a secure job with the school district and a cocaine habit. He thought about things. He liked to talk about the things he thought about. This habit caused him no end of trouble with the staff.

Besides thinking, Daniel read books, practiced yoga, and struggled with the mysteries of life. He brought to these struggles an odd strength of character. He seemed to have no envy and no desire for wealth. He had been able to teach children without becoming childish himself. His interest in ideas, however, was just a bit too public. People tired of him easily, and once tired by one of his discourses, seldom took the time to listen to him again.

That evening he was struggling with why he was unable to control the mock AA meeting. Big John maintained that there had to be fire and brimstone or no one would pay attention. I suggested as I often did to Daniel that he had to keep things simpler. "We're here about drinking and drugging," I told him, "not about our conception of God. Common sense says you get people to talk about drinking, not religion."

"Do you have common sense?" he asked.

"I don't know, I guess so," I said.

"Some people have common sense and some don't. Those who have it tend to be smug about it. Those who don't have it spend their lives being envious of those who do. I am one of the envious ones." I glanced at Big John, who rolled his eyes. "Everyday problems evaporate in the face of common sense. With it a person can fix a sink, drive places without a map, and effortlessly complete a myriad of tasks that completely bewilder those of us who don't have it. Common sense smoothes the bumps in the road of life, and I was born without it.

"Lacking common sense, I am an object of pity to my common sensible friends and relatives. They shake their heads and look at the floor when they speak of my handicap. They assure me that I can still enjoy a full life. I'd rather have cancer.

"I've studied common sense. Common sense is bestowed upon people in licks. I don't have a lick of common sense. I have an uncle who has seven licks of the stuff. That makes him the common sense equivalent of a genius. Common sense is unrelated to race, religion, or national origin. However, women have more than men, and there are some who say it is very uncommon among the French. Common sense prevents people from remaining poor, but seldom makes them rich, unless, of course, they have the common sense to inherit well.

"Science has yet to determine whether common sense is a product of heredity or environment. The heredity argument is undercut by the indisputable fact that fathers always have more common sense than their sons. Adherents of the environmental argument are hindered by the fact that children reared around people with high levels of common sense either run away from home early or suffer from varying degrees of mental illness. My own addiction, I suspect, is partially a result of being raised in a home that was high in common sense. The religious community has yet to take a consistent position but most religions hold that common sense has something or other to do with God.

No thorough study, to my knowledge, has ever been done on common sense in identical twins.

"Medical, psychological, and educational institutions have given the subject of common sense remarkably little attention. No public or private college that I know of offers even an introductory course in the subject. The teachers I have questioned allege that although educators possess a high degree of common sense, there is no pedagogical avenue by which it can be transferred to students. The Portland Public Library contains fourteen titles on how to repair air conditioners, but not a single volume explaining common sense. Every psychologist I questioned suggested I go to a different discipline, and some admitted quite candidly that psychologists were not generally well endowed with the quality. The only medical doctor I know who has addressed the issue suggested that common sense has something to do with the four food groups and moderation in all things.

"Those of us who must get along without common sense receive plenty of sympathy, but very little actual help. Every other handicap has a political action group, a special Olympic program, and several university medical centers spending boatloads of federal money looking for solutions. A person who lacks common sense has nowhere to turn.

"The reason for the lack of interest in this problem is twofold. The first is denial. Like the illiterate, or we alcoholics, the person lacking common sense hides his handicap from himself and others. He becomes the consummate pretender. He browses in the nail section of hardware stores. He hides cookbooks and claims to cook without a recipe. He buys dental floss in bulk. As a result of this denial, those without common sense are unable to effectively organize. The second reason is that the doers and shakers of society, the politicians, artists, and philanthropists who serve as the catalysts in movements to help the needy, lack the commons sense to see the problem. For these reasons the movement to help the common senseless is without either leaders or followers. That is no way to make progress."

He stopped. Big John and I looked at him and then each other in awe. "Is that the end, professor?" I asked.

"I can continue," he responded.

"No, no thanks," I said. "I feel educated enough for tonight."

"So what is the answer?" Big John asked.

"I didn't know there was a question," Daniel said.

"How can people with no common sense get help?"

"They can't. They just live with it. They pray for a miracle."

6

The Christmas without the socks was forgiven but not forgotten. Alcohol and marijuana had brought Isol and me together. In the months following that Christmas it began tearing us apart. Drink is a jealous lover; it accepts no rivals.

The rest of the winter months passed without any significant changes in our lives. My hands developed a permanent shake. My body acquired an odor of alcohol that could not be showered away. Isol worked during the day and tried to drink away the desperation of our situation at night. I just drank.

At some point during that year alcohol quit working. I no longer felt good when I drank; I no longer got high. The escape and elation that I had fallen in love with the first time I drank was gone. All the liquor could do was deaden the pain.

I drank to get to a place I knew as the zone, a place just the other side of living. It was easy to get there and easy to stay there. Three beers put me there and once in the zone, it didn't take much maintenance to keep me there. The zone was a foggy place where things moved slowly. Time was uneven and unpredictable. There was white noise, like the sound of the ocean you get from a sea shell, which muted the sounds of the real world. Moving around in the zone felt like I was walking in mud. Spirits lived there. Being in the zone didn't prevent me from doing the shopping and the other little chores that I still did to keep up the façade of a normal life, but it made those things into dreams.

Regular people couldn't tell when I was in the zone, or if they could, they never said anything about it.

I was losing weight and vomiting every morning. The black sandy material in my vomit was the coagulated blood from my bleeding stomach. I seldom ate, and I had to grip my morning cup of coffee with both hands in order to get it to my lips.

Everything outside the apartment was the enemy. Going to the post office to mail my unemployment forms took all the energy and will power I could muster. A bus trip to the law library exhausted me.

Surviving in the zone required me to blank out any vision of the future that extended beyond the day immediately in front of me. Surviving the day was all that mattered. In the zone actions lacked consequences beyond the moment. Problems were immediate, so putting them off was the same as solving them and tomorrow became the depository for every difficulty. I had learned to live *one day at a time* in the most desperate sense of the phrase.

I made it through by lying. I'd lie to cover up the lies I'd told the day before, and I lied just to be lying. Everything I said and did was a lie. Once a person has woven a fabric of lies, even a little bit of truth mixed in infects the weave. For purity's sake, I eliminated the truth.

I sometimes looked for work during the week, but more often than not I would fill out my unemployment forms by going through the phone book for business addresses where I could claim to have applied. I lied on the few applications I managed to fill out. If I got an interview, I lied to the interviewer. When I got to Taps, I lied to the Lemmings and the barkeeps. Each of the Lemmings pursued alcoholism in his or her own way, but I was the only one paralyzed by it. The other Lemmings kept their jobs, paid their bills, and maintained some sort of life away from Taps. I did none of those things, so I lied instead. I told the barkeeps I was doing legal research on a contract basis so I could explain being able to show up at Taps every afternoon before anyone else was off work. I told the Lemmings I was on the verge of being hired by a law firm, or maybe the county, or a title company. It didn't matter, as long as the lie worked for that day. In the zone, if the lie worked for one day, it worked forever.

I lied to Isol. The grinding weight of my addiction was slowly smothering her. She faced the same thing every day: the bills we couldn't pay, the undone dishes, the grocery bags of empty beer cans piled on the kitchen floor. She had the job of hiding the elephant of addiction that we kept in the living room. When relatives, coworkers, or even friends showed up in our private life, it was her job to prop up the facade of normalcy. With little to work with she did a marvelous job. Determined at all costs to protect us as a family, she was able to call on some primeval strength, not only to prevent the addiction from tearing us apart, but also to hold up that wall which shielded us from prying eyes.

When the weekends came alcohol was not enough. We had always smoked pot while drinking, but after a while even the two together couldn't bring back the old times. In the zone there is no getting high no matter how much you drink. I wanted the fun back. For a while, cocaine provided relief. Cocaine took me out of the dull sameness of the zone. It meant fun, camaraderie, and sex. For a while, on cocaine, I enjoyed drinking again. I drew pictures and painted, but the effect of cocaine is short lived, and when it wears off you are only poorer.

That summer we had no money for camping or golf. Paying the rent and paying the bill at Taps took every penny we had. The drinking and drugs no longer brought us together. When Isol and I came home from our Friday night binges we would fight bitterly into the wee hours of the morning. The battles were long and vicious.

"Get a fuckin' job," she would scream. "I can't take this shit any more." I would withdraw into the zone to hide. I couldn't fight back. I was guilty of all the accusations and more. Once Isol had screamed herself into exhaustion she would collapse on the bed. I would drink away the guilt and then walk the early morning streets. Sometimes, I'd go for pancakes and sausage. Sometimes I'd go to the park with a basketball and shoot free throws until the sun rose and I could sleep. Sometimes I would substitute a pot of coffee for a night's rest and start drinking again.

That fall my parents received a financial windfall and shared a few thousand dollars with Isol and me. The money held off our creditors and put food in the refrigerator. At Christmas there was good vodka in the freezer and a pair of socks beneath the tree. We went to

Taps for New Years Eve and partied with the Lemmings. I celebrated the New Year with a sense of relief. I had decided it would be my last.

The money from my parents ran out. I was in the zone and couldn't get out. I bought beer I didn't want to buy. I opened cans I didn't want to open, and drank when I didn't want to drink. I drank beer for breakfast—lots of it. It didn't matter any more. I'd sit with my Budweiser watching Marx Brothers movies and planning my suicide. I had lost everything. I had destroyed any future that Isol and I might have had, and now that everything was gone except our love, I was destroying that. Without ever meaning to, I had become evil.

My body was failing rapidly. I had constant diarrhea, and anything except alcohol made me vomit. My hands shook all the time. Occasionally, I tried, one drink at a time, to stop myself from going to the kitchen for the next beer, but I physically could not stop myself.

I told Isol that I'd gotten a job. I made up an office, coworkers, a boss and an income. They were all lies. Like getting another drink from the kitchen, I didn't know why I did it. I would put on a shirt and tie in the morning as if I were going to work. Instead of going, I would walk around the block and return to the apartment to drink and plan my suicide. The inner me, rather than being the source of my behaviors, became an observer of the things I did, and those things disgusted me. The me inside was getting weaker by the day. I had to kill the body.

I'd planned for my death to occur some time before my first imaginary paycheck became due. Selfish to the end, I wanted to spare myself one final humiliation of telling Isol there was no job. Death would free me from the lies. My body would stop hurting people and my pain would end. Isol would be left with the mess and the funeral expenses, however, after the trauma she would be better off. She would find someone who didn't destroy everything he touched.

I never came seriously close to killing myself. Alcohol controlled me, and it didn't want me to die. Broken, I reached out instead. Isol was the only person who knew I was still in there somewhere. I asked her to help.

7

After reviewing my test results, Wayne, my counselor told me, "You're a garden variety alcoholic. You suffer from depression, but the depression is situational, not chronic." Although it did somewhat limit what he could bill my insurance, Wayne considered this good news. I was disappointed. I'd hoped for a rare form of the disease special to me.

Wayne was a pleasant counselor. Once athletic, he had become overweight and slow moving. His addiction had taken him through a smorgasbord of drugs, but it was methamphetamine in a syringe that did him in. His laid back approach to counseling struck me as being an extreme counterpoint of what he must have been like on speed. Both of us liked golf. We spent a good portion of the counseling sessions lying to each other about our golf games.

Wayne kept the ring binder I saw on my first day at the Manor. He worked diligently at keeping the binder complete and seemed comfortably confident that if the binder was up to date, everything else would fall into place. In our first meeting Wayne told me that alcohol treatment programs had the lowest rate of success with alcohol counselors and lawyers. Alcohol counselors were tough because, knowing the program so intimately, they had an intellectual resistance to it. Lawyers were tough because they turned every situation adversarial. The made the process into the lawyer versus treatment, and the lawyer usually won.

"You have more formal education and more raw

intelligence than I do," Wayne told me while staring at my test results. I was flattered, but education and intelligence hadn't done a whit to keep me from becoming a drunk. "I feel that I can't say anything that you haven't already heard," he said. "I'm normally good at reading people. I can see progress, see changes, by the look in a person's eyes, but you look me straight in the eye, and I see nothing. I don't know if you hear me when I talk."

I did hear him. I was listening. I knew that only one person in ten at the Manor would stay clean for a year. I wanted sobriety, and he was offering it. I watched him and listened to him. Education and intelligence had nothing to do with it. If I could have, I would have sucked the sobriety out of him like a vampire sucking blood. I wouldn't have cared if he were left a derelict in the process. I needed what he had. Wayne mistook my covetousness for inscrutability.

"Your treatment," Wayne said, "will consist of building self esteem and reducing denial. Does that sound all right to you?" He always explained and then asked permission.

"Sure," I said. What was I supposed to say? He gave me several writing assignments to present in group. The assignments were one page photocopied sets of questions that resembled the kind of homework I'd gotten in the fifth grade. "Name ten qualities you like about yourself; name ten things other people like about you." The page had numbers down the left side with blanks for the answers.

Wayne liked my drawings. Once my hands stopped

shaking, I'd used spare time or dull portions of lectures to draw little cartoons about life at the Manor. Each of the cartoons was a caricature of myself doing some aspect of the Manor routine. When I showed them to Wayne he blossomed. I explained that I'd been drawing as long as I could remember. More than one client had been startled to find, after a long recess in a trial, a caricature of the judge adorning the legal pad at counsel table. One of my drawings published in my law school newspaper, a caricature of a particularly vain professor, attracted enough attention to endanger my continued welcome at the school. The drawings I did at the Manor were not vicious. They were snippets of the funny side of the Manor. In a burst of counseling creativity, Wayne decided that artwork should be part of my therapy. He assigned me to make one drawing a day and to turn the drawing in to him. The assignment resulted in the worst case of artist block I have ever experienced.

I presented my self-esteem assignment, and all other assignments, in group. The lectures and movies we endured at the Manor were recreation. Group was the working part of the day. For group, we broke up into randomly selected sets of from six to ten patients and for ninety minutes, six days a week, examined our feelings, our drugs, and the behaviors that stemmed from both. We dished up our angers, guilt, and resentments like mashed potatoes at Christmas dinner. The smoking room was our place to laugh. Group was the place to cry.

Addicts don't trust anyone. They've never been

trustworthy themselves so there is no reason for them to believe that other people are any different. Using dishonesty as a survival mechanism each of us had created a persona separate from ourselves. This other person, built of lies, was the person we presented to the world. By hiding our real selves we avoided being judged. Everyone started in group presenting the other self—the self built from lies.

The facades we built to show the world were stereotypes: the tough guy, the iconoclast, the intellectual, the artist, the victim. No one was original. Our characters were stolen from books or television; they were roles to play, but our tough guys were afraid, our artists produced no art and our victims were their own oppressors.

Little by little we began to talk truthfully about the life of addiction. As it turned out, not only were the lies we told to hide our addictions all the same, but so were the desperate lives we really lived. Our addictions were identical. Cocaine in a Mercedes is only a few dollars away from wine in a paper bag. It is addiction—predictable, boring, and fatal.

When an alkie or addict is high he knows how the rain ought to fall, how the sun ought to shine. He is the source of all knowledge. He imposes order on the universe. In the depth of the depression that follows heavy use, he feels himself the most evil and despicable soul ever to walk among the living—his lies are the worst, his crimes the most heinous. The lows push us toward suicide. Some of us do it; most don't. In group we learned from each other that our crimes were petty and unimaginative. We weren't special and we weren't evil. We were average people, addicted people, sitting in a circle talking about unspectacular problems.

Group made me feel good about all the things I hadn't done wrong. I'd lost a house and a career, but I hadn't seen the inside of a prison. I'd always slept in a bed. Others were not as lucky. We had each hit bottom in a different place, but bottom is the same for everyone. Bottom is desperation and self-loathing; it is a state of mind that can occur in a lot of different locations.

Addiction is fatal but not entertaining over any significant period of time. Seeing it in another is like watching a person die of athlete's foot: slow, tedious, and disgusting. Remove the addictions, however, and you have average people. I have always found average people interesting. In group I grew to like the average people beneath the addictions, and they came to tolerate me.

On Saturdays we had lifeline. During lifeline all of the patients met in the meditation room. Once we were together, one of the patients would take a half-hour or so to tell the story of his or her life. The stories were supposed to include the good, the bad, and the ugly. The stories varied, but each ending was the same. They all ended in addiction and a trip through the front door of the Manor.

When I first arrived at the Manor I couldn't tell the truth about what I'd done the previous week, so when I first sat through lifeline, I cried. I cried because I saw my disease in others. I also cried because I would never possess the strength to truthfully tell my story to any person, much less a room full of strangers. Wayne and I went round after round about this. I wanted to talk about Isol—how much I loved her—how much I wanted to make up for what I had done. Wayne wanted to talk about me. He wanted to hear how I felt about myself and what I was willing to do for myself. In group I could usually deflect attention from me by being helpful and supportive to others. I avoided me. Wayne would have none of it. He wanted to know what I felt. I couldn't tell him because without alcohol I didn't feel anything.

Meetings with our counselors were known as one-on-one. For a while mine turned into him on me. He wanted to talk about me. He wanted to know where I came from and how I got from there to the Manor. He wanted to find some emotion left inside of me. I wanted to talk about sports.

Wayne made me write out the complete history of my drug and alcohol use starting with my first drink. It was an interesting monograph. I presented it in group and even the other alkies were amazed. For a day or so I was a bit of a cult hero based upon my ability to physically survive such abuse. The body is an amazing thing.

Daniel was in my group the day I delivered my litany of drug and alcohol use.

"The sixties were good to you," he volunteered after group.

"Yeah," I told him, "for me they ended in 1979."

"I was a flower child myself."

"I bet you were good at it, though. I failed as a hippie."

"How can you fail as a hippie?" he asked.

"I grew long hair. I sewed paisley inserts in my bell-bottoms. I protested war. My best friend was one of the most popular hippies on campus. I walked into his apartment one day unannounced while he and some others were smoking dope and playing bluegrass. As I stepped into the room they hid the marijuana. My hair and beads didn't fool them. They were enlightened. I was an addict."

"That's a sad story," Daniel said.

"I bet you were a good hippie?"

"The best. Communes, maharishis, enlightenment, the whole nine yards."

"Did you take LSD and see God?"

"All the time."

"So what happened?"

"I was going to Reed College, riding home from school on my bike when a car pulled out. I flew and cracked my head. I was in the hospital for a week. I never went back to school. A year later I grabbed a quick teaching degree from Portland State and got a job."

"At least you kept the job."

"Public employment," he said, "always forgiving, great insurance."

"So what happened to enlightenment?"

"Any day now," he said.

Wayne had little success at getting me to open up. To spur me forward he made me write down ten feelings every day. When I felt an emotion—anger, pleasure, pain—I was supposed to write it down. I had to turn in my list of feelings every day. Under the gun to have at least ten a day, I walked around the Manor, notebook in hand, alert for feelings. Someone on the staff irritated me, ah, jot it down. One of the patients compliments me on one of my drawings and I feel proud. Jot it down.

The point of the feelings list was to get me to the overflowing cauldron of guilt that I carried inside me. I, like most of the other inmates, had cut a path of destruction on the road to the Manor. Injured souls and lost opportunities littered the roadway. On the outside I suppressed the guilt by self-medication. In the Manor I resurrected the Nordic stoicism and concepts of self-reliance impressed upon me in childhood. This kept the guilt and all my other emotions at bay. As days went by, filling the notebook became easier. I began to recognize little feelings. Big ones, however, would have to wait.

After three days in the infirmary, Stevie appeared. She came into dinner wearing a bathrobe and fuzzy slippers. She nibbled at food and left in the middle of her meal to throw up. After dinner she appeared in the smoking room wearing the same outfit. She didn't remember anyone from the first day.

"How are you feeling?" I asked.

"Do I know you?" she responded.

"We met when you first came in."

"Oh, great," she responded. I introduced myself. "So what do we do for fun here?" she asked. "Irritate the staff?"

"We smoke," I answered.

"Does that irritate the staff?"

"Not really."

"So what's the plan then?" Stevie was sober. She spent the rest of the day playing competitive solitaire with a couple of the other patients and recruiting commandos for the plan.

On Sunday I was off isolation and permitted visitors between one and four o'clock in the afternoon. Each patient made out a guest list, and only people on the list were permitted through the front door. When a guest arrived the patient was summoned from the dorm. For people with visitors, Sunday was a reminder that the difficulties outside were still there waiting. For those without visitors, it was a reminder of their loneliness.

I was nervous. Isol was on the list—so were some of the Lemmings. Isol arrived promptly at one o'clock. I first saw her standing in the lobby looking nervous and afraid. We hugged. We held hands.

I took Isol on a tour of the downstairs amenities. She was not permitted in the dorm. We shared a cup of coffee in the dining room. The conversation was hesitant and superficial.

"How are the Lemmings?"

"They're fine. They won't be coming though. They call a lot. Angie has been bringing over dinner."

"How's work?"

"Fine. Are you okay here?"

"I'm fine."

"Are you sure?"

"I'm fine," I repeated. Tears welled in her eyes.

"I miss you."

"I miss you too."

"I've been cleaning the apartment."

"That's good."

"Are you sure you're okay."

"I'm fine."

"Do you still love me?"

"I still love you," I assured her. "Are you surviving this?"

"It's hard."

Facing big changes, we could only speak of small things. Each of us was going through a transformation and neither knew how the other would emerge when it was done. Our past, built upon drugs, was evaporating and our future was empty. We faced a life and a love that had to be built anew. It was too early to know if we could do that. We were paralyzed in the present. Isol was afraid, and she cried. I felt numb. I went through the motions of comforting her, trying to be reassuring, but my feelings about her were too big. I knew where I was, and that was progress. I couldn't yet think about where I was going.

8

Malady Manor had a ghost. The ghost lived on the deserted third floor and was sometimes seen in an unused wing that had once been an infirmary. At times patients would catch a glimpse of him in one of the eight gabled windows that extended from the roof of the Manor. During the day he stayed hidden. At night he visited the patients.

"He looks like Colonel Sanders," Stevie said. "I woke up in the middle of my second night, down in the infirmary. He was standing in the door to my room holding a little dog."

"Did you ask for some hair of the dog?" Big John responded.

"I'm serious," she said. "He was standing there and then he was gone."

"I haven't seen him," I said, "but he closed my window. When I first got here the window in my room wouldn't open because of the ivy. A couple days ago I finally got it open. That afternoon I was getting ready for bed and the window just closed. It didn't fall shut— it couldn't, because of the ivy—it closed. Slowly and carefully, it shut itself."

Daniel came into the room to listen. Someone was telling about the basement door that couldn't be propped open. The ghost kept closing it.

"Do you believe in ghosts, Daniel?" Big John asked.

"No," he said. He didn't want to discuss it.

Jack, the silent Indian, had been standing alone

against one wall, seemingly oblivious to the conversation around him. He walked to the door. Before leaving he turned to us and said to no one in particular, "The ghost is a white man."

"I knew that," Stevie said.

The Manor had been built in the nineteen twenties. Originally a retirement home for the wealthy widows of the city, the furnishings on the ground floor still had the scent of elderly females with money. The retirement home closed in the fifties and the building was empty for twenty-five years. In the seventies it was refurbished and reopened as a drug and alcohol treatment center. During the remodel, the basement and first two floors were rewired and re-plumbed for modern habitability. The dorm area was furnished with used motel furniture, but the top floor and the infirmary were left mostly empty.

The top floor was built like our dorm floor except the windows in the rooms were the gabled windows that extended from the long roof. The third floor was off limits to the patients—the stairways blocked, theater style, with velvet ropes.

The infirmary wing was a one-story addition to the building extending to the north. The wing had enough room for a good-sized medical clinic, but the Manor had only opened up three small rooms to be used for patients who needed isolation or observation. The remainder of the wing was empty. We theorized that in the days of the retirement home the residents went to the infirmary to die. We called it the death house.

"C'mon Daniel," John said, "you're a spiritual sort

of guy. You must believe in spirits."

"I believe in ghosts," Stevie declared, "because I plan to be one, especially if I can have a dog."

"Don't you have to die before your time, or something like that?" I asked.

"Oh, I'll do that," she said. "Then I'll haunt people. I'll haunt my real estate office and screw up deals. My ghost dog will pee on the closing papers."

"My Aunt Eva told me dogs don't have souls," I said. "They can't go to heaven so they can't be ghosts either."

"She got it wrong. Only dogs go to heaven. People become ghosts or go to hell, but some dogs stick around a while as ghosts to keep human ghosts company."

"You should tell Sky Pilot about all that," Daniel suggested.

She whispered, "I did."

I had my own theories about the ghost. I imagined him the live-in manager at the old retirement home. He had lived with his dog in one of the third floor rooms and spent his days tending to the needs of the ladies. I could see him having tea with his well-dressed and educated wards. I imagined him having a room on the top floor, above the world, safe and warm so he never had to leave the Manor. Quiet and serene, his room was above the turmoil of the city. The ladies died or moved away. The Manor closed, but he stayed in his room, safe from everything. Now that the Manor had re-opened, he wandered the halls closing windows and doors to keep the outside out.

In the last years of my addiction I seldom slept in the normal sense of the word. When sober I was usually in some version of race brain; fear of tomorrow and the regrets of yesterday squeezed out the present. In order to rest I medicated myself and imagined a room in a storm. Outside, wind blew and waves crashed against the rocks, but inside I was warm and safe. I invented a storm to find peace, and when I could find peace, I could steal a few hours of dreamless sleep.

There were dreams aplenty at the Manor. The dreams brought the ghost down into the dorm. After years of drugged unconsciousness instead of sleep, addicts become plagued by dreams. I was tortured by them. In the dreams I was back in the zone. I was frantically hiding my beer cans or trying to wash away the odor of whiskey. The dreams were so real that upon awakening it would take me several minutes to realize where I was. One by one, I would review the events of the previous twenty-four hours to convince myself that what happened in the dream was not real. Some times I'd wake up at night and escape the dreams by wandering the Manor. I'd go out into the hall where Aaron, the giant, would be peacefully asleep at his desk, then to the smoking room for a cigarette. The Manor was silent, and I could feel the collective nightmares of the sleeping patients. Then I felt the presence of the ghost.

I'd never given the slightest credence to the occult, however, when sitting among the drug dreams of the other patients, I became willing to believe. Alone in the smoking room the ghost was real. I remembered Alice and the White Queen. "One can't believe impossible things," Alice told her.

"I daresay you haven't had much practice," said the Queen. "When I was your age I did it for half-an-hour a day. Why, sometimes I've believed as many as six impossible things before breakfast."

9

Each of our counselors had to possess ten hours of recovery-related lectures in order to maintain government certification. They practiced on us every morning from ten to eleven. In these presentations we learned how drugs worked, why people took them, and where we ended up when we took too many. We were lectured about AID's, anger control, and a host of disgusting degenerative diseases related to drug use. The scientific information was accurate and up-to-date. Having been a drinker and smoker for years, I ignored it all.

Logic is useless against addiction. The straight world will never truly understand this. Those who try to reason with an addict to stop him from using are destined to loneliness and frustration. However, the barrage of scientific claptrap I had to endure from the counselors had an effect. It brought me to the point where I understood that the traditional methods of analysis, deduction, and conclusion were not my friends when it came to drugs. I would need to find the proper thought processes elsewhere.

In the evening we had speakers from local AA groups. Unlike the doctors and psychologists, the speakers spoke the language of the addict. Each, in his own way, had plumbed the depths of addiction and had come out alive. These speakers never gave us statistics and never told us what to do. They simply told their stories. They did not instruct or reason with us. In telling their stories they could touch us in a place that no lecturer could ever reach. After several of these experiences I came to the conclusion that a straight person would never be able to help me with addiction, but maybe, just maybe, another alcoholic could.

On Saturday nights, instead of a speaker, a trusted few of the patients were selected to attend an outside AA meeting. My turn to go came on my second Saturday in treatment. Cowboy Bob herded us into the Manor parking lot and then into the van. With ten backseat drivers he headed to the city center. I sat next to Big John. As we left the grounds the sights of the city felt new to me. The streets were wet, reflecting the lights off the pavement. I took up my feelings notebook and wrote the word, "awe."

I tried to look into tavern windows as the van passed them on the street. The soft glow of neon in the rain called to me. I knew that inside those places the barroom was warm and the beer was cold. Friends I didn't know yet were waiting for me.

Diminutive Cowboy Bob suffered a barrage of abuse as he drove. "Hey Bob," my roommate Robert yelled, "can you see out the windshield and still reach the pedals."

"Stop at McDonalds," ordered another of the riders.

"A titty bar, then McDonalds."

"Hey Bob, let's go to California."

"Bob can't go to California, they check for short people at the border."

"Everyone shut up," Bob yelled. The order produced a round of boos.

At a stop light an elderly couple in a Mercedes

pulled up next to us. Robert yelled, "Straight people. Let's kill them." Those of us with window seats pressed our faces against the glass to scare away the straights.

Our drunkmobile eventually pulled into the parking lot of a large building situated behind a strip mall. The parking lot was crowded, and the front door was partially blocked by a collection of Harley Davidsons. We climbed out of the van into the rain and stood there waiting for Bob to tell us what to do.

"Well, go on in," he said. He headed across the lot toward the door and we all followed.

The door led to an AA social club. We entered a large smoky room filled with card players, pool shooters, and pinball machines. It looked like a tavern, but instead of beer, they did a brisk business in soda, salty snacks, and candy bars. Families, teens, senior citizens, hippies, bikers, blacks, whites, and dogs mixed in the crowd. Sobriety, I thought, brings with it a tolerance seldom seen in taverns. These people had not done their drinking together.

I didn't like the club. Alcoholics who didn't drink disturbed me, particularly when they did their non-drinking together and in public. I was embarrassed for them, but they weren't embarrassed for themselves. I stayed close to my Manor buddies. We bought large caffeine-laden soda pops at the snack bar and found a table at the edge of the room. No one talked.

Shortly before seven thirty, Cowboy Bob herded us into an adjoining room filled with tables and chairs arranged in a loose semicircle around a small desk. My Manor comrades and I took seats at a table to one side of the room while Cowboy Bob wandered off to see friends. The regulars eyed us suspiciously. Volunteers wandered among the tables pouring coffee. My baptism into real AA was about to begin.

An older man took a seat at the desk in front. He called the meeting to order and then called on people to read the Twelve Traditions and How it Works, readings from the Big Book. He spoke for a few minutes about his own battle with alcohol and then called on others to share.

In turn, each of the people called upon related his or her struggles with addiction and struggles in sobriety. The speakers weren't counselors, apprentice counselors, ministers, or psychologists. They were regular Joes and Josephines speaking honestly about their personal recoveries from addiction. One would pound the table like a Mississippi evangelist. The next might speak softly, like a mother to her child. Some dressed like longshoremen. Others wore white shirts and ties. Each spoke of struggle and salvation, and every one of them was sober.

I was astonished and envious. I wasn't surprised that some people had sacrificed more of their lives to drugs than I. I was surprised that they could talk about it. They weren't shy, remorseful, or ashamed. They told stories of defeat at the hands of drug abuse, but each one was proud—proud that he or she had not used drugs or alcohol that day. For most of them, the one day at a times had turned into years. I wanted what they had.

At the end of the meeting the crowd formed a

crooked circle and, holding hands, said the Lord's Prayer. I was still embarrassed by the private things that had been said and uneasy about the references to God that had punctuated so many of the stories, but as a whole, the meeting had been electric. For a long time I had felt as if there was nothing new in the world for me. What I had seen in the meeting was new.

Filled with coffee and soda pop, we sloshed our way out of the meeting and back to the van. Cowboy Bob had us back to the Manor before ten.

Conversation in the smoking room was slow that night. We compared favorites among the people who had spoken at the meeting. We talked about having real coffee, but no one talked about what really happened there. I had seen a different world, a strange culture within a culture. I didn't know what to think about it, but I felt intuitively that somehow my life depended on what I had seen.

10

After a week at the Manor I decided to give in and actually read the Big Book. I had resisted doing so precisely because the staff was always on my case to do it. All I heard from them was, "The Big Book says this," and "The Big Book says that." Against my better judgment and in violation of the unwritten rule that all staff suggestions should be ignored, I started to read.

In the beginning I didn't want any of the other patients to see me reading the book, so I hid away in a seldom used basement lounge. There I could smoke, drink decaffeinated coffee, and read. Sober for over a week and well fed, I was as open to new learning as a person with too much college can ever be.

The book had stories. It begins with the story of Bill W., the founder of AA. Bill was a man who knew how to drink. The book had a lot of other people's stories too, all of whom were drunks. In the Big Book, however, the drunks end up sober.

In addition to stories about drunks, the book had a system for getting sober and living sober. The system didn't depend upon psychiatry, piety, or penance. It didn't rely on miracle drugs or miracles. Instead, it laid out twelve steps. Although AA and the Twelve Steps had been around for forty years, as I sat there in the basement of the Manor all of it was new to me. The book described clearly and completely the program that the Manor staff had been trying to spoon feed us in bits and pieces. I finished the book in two sittings. What was in that book was what the people at the Saturday night AA meeting already knew. It was what had kept them sober.

I decided to tackle the steps. Actually, everything at the Manor was designed to get patients to take the steps. However, doing them takes a certain amount of personal resolve and a modicum of courage. Food, exercise, and numbing routine cannot make a person take the steps, but they provide physical strength and boredom sufficient to put a person in the mood. In that deserted basement lounge I gave it a try.

The first step was admitting powerlessness over alcohol. To quote the book, "We admitted we were powerless over alcohol—that out lives had become unmanageable." I reasoned that this step was easy. Hadn't I checked into the Manor because I couldn't handle alcohol? There, I was powerless over alcohol. I admitted it. Furthermore, my life had become unmanageable. I was spending my days locked up and going from room to room at the sound of a bell. If that wasn't unmanageable, I didn't know what was. So in a minute I had passed step one. I felt ready to start my own treatment center.

After an hour or so with Wayne I had to reevaluate. He convinced me that my approach to step one was a bit simplistic. He loaded me down with a long list of questions about drinking in my life. All the questions required essay answers.

I wrote page after page of answers to Wayne's questions in my notebook. I chronicled my drug use, my feeble efforts to curtail drinking, and the effect that drugs and alcohol had on my life. The writing was difficult at first because the assignment required me to put down on paper things that I preferred not to even think about. With each page, however, the going got easier.

The work on step one was supposed to help me overcome denial. I'd learned about denial from several annoying lecturers who smugly proclaimed that a symptom of addiction was a persistent denial by the afflicted person that he or she had a problem. I had never thought much of the problem approach. Losing one's keys is a problem. A problem can be solved or ignored, depending on how much it bothers you. Alcoholism is more than a problem. It devours a person, his possessions, and all those around him. Step one, for me, wasn't admitting I had a problem; my appearance among the patients at Malady Manor proved that. Step one was accepting that my life was controlled and dominated by alcohol, that my addiction was destroying everything around me, and that there was absolutely nothing I could do about it.

Doing my first step brought back seriously unpleasant memories. I wrote about hiding my liquor, lying about my drug use, and fighting hangovers in the courtroom. Of all the memories, I remembered most vividly those mornings in my apartment when I tried to force myself not to drink until noon. I'd go to the kitchen for coffee and come back with a beer. It was seven o'clock in the morning and I was drinking again.

Despite the overwhelming written evidence, admitting powerlessness still turned out to be difficult for me. Powerlessness is un-American. Having grown up on Emerson, John Wayne, and the pioneer ideal of self-reliance, I was not inclined to accept the idea that anything controlled me. What I needed was some good food, some confidence, and a stiff shot of will power. I'd heard the lectures and seen the films. I knew exactly how and why drugs were killing me. I had a good wife to support me, and the basic intelligence to see what needed to change. I could assert myself by making different and better choices. And, I had thought all these things a thousand times before, only to end up drunk before noon.

As the pages filled up in my notebook, the person who emerged was no John Wayne. It dawned on me that if I could get sober with a stiff shot of will power and Nordic resolve, I might have done it years ago. On the other hand, I had been awfully busy during those two decades. I had more time for will power now that I didn't have a house, a car, or a job to distract me. Wayne reviewed my first step jottings with the interest of a flight attendant reading emergency procedures. My meeting with him reminded me that no matter how dramatic all this was to me, the disease is seldom entertaining to others.

"How do you think you are doing?" Wayne would ask. I didn't know. He was the expert. I wanted him to read what I had to say and give me an "A."

"I don't know," I'd tell him. "The step is a trap. How can you overcome something by giving in to it. I feel locked in a closet." He would nod and write a few notes in my file.

I knew from the lectures and films that alcoholism

would continue to progress even if I never drank again. Should I quit for five years and start again I would not be picking up where I left off. I would react as if I had been drinking as heavily as ever throughout the period of sobriety. The disease continues, even when you do not drink. I understood powerlessness in that strict scientific sense, but acceptance of complete and utter defeat not only went against my nature, it was embarrassing.

I vacillated in and out of accepting my addiction. However, having to write out the history of drugs in my life put my drug use physically in front of me. All the drinking and drugging was now on paper. The lost jobs, lost friends, and wasted opportunities were down on yellow tablets where I could walk away from them. They were still part of me, but they weren't all that I was.

I did my writing in the smoking room. While I worked on step one, others did their own assignments. We had a lot of writing going on. Doing steps at the Manor was like doing high school book reports. You wrote your stuff, got a grade, and moved on to the next one. Because insurance only covered a certain number of days, nobody failed. The program at the Manor was the Cliff Notes version of Alcoholics Anonymous.

The approaches to the steps varied as much as the patients themselves. Daniel and I wrote page after page on the more-is-better theory. Others resorted to haiku on the less-is-easier theory. Some refused to do it at all until they learned that if they didn't, they had to reimburse the insurance company for the Manor charges.

"So have you overcome denial?" I asked Stevie during one of those breaks in the writing when we lied to each other about how well it was all going.

"I think so," she said. "I'm a drug addict. I'll always be a drug addict. That's it, isn't it." Stevie personified action to me in the way that Daniel personified intellect.

"What about powerlessness. Admitting defeat, can you do that?" I asked.

"Yeah. I've been whipped before," she said. "I don't get mad. I get even."

"And how do you get even with the habit."

"I'm gonna live one hell of a life when I get straight."

11

On Sunday after the real AA meeting, we had an easy schedule and ample time to fret about the arrival of our afternoon visitors. After breakfast and meditation I settled into a chair in the television room to watch some basketball. My roommate Robert and a couple of the other young inmates joined me. Indian Jack sat in one corner, but didn't join in conversation or appear to be interested in the game. As the game progressed more of Robert's friends wandered in.

Seven or eight of the Manor patients were young men in their early twenties. Drawn to each other, they sat together at meals, supported each other in group, and constituted a distinct subgroup among the patients. They had named themselves the Barracudas, a reference to the table manners they exhibited in the dining room.

I was jealous of these young men. They had a chance to kick their addictions early—before they had sacrificed twenty years to drugs—yet they confused me. A person usually hits some sort of bottom to get to the Manor. For me the bottom had been paralysis, the taste of death, and days on end in the zone. When I came in I was physically beaten. The barracudas came in strong and arrogant. Fueled by testosterone and a profound ignorance of the world, they pushed through each day with blinding energy. They hadn't been to the zone, and they were still physically able to get high. They had so much future to be afraid of and so few tools for surviving the real world that I wondered why any of them would want to do it without drugs.

During the basketball game Robert rooted for the Portland team with his friend Rollo. Unlike most of the young men at the Manor, both Robert and Rollo came from wealthy families and both had managed to achieve some economic success in their short lives. Robert, in addition to snorting up his $100,000 insurance settlement, was a union machinist. His skill commanded twenty dollars an hour any time he chose to work. Rollo happened into a job on the ground floor of a local sports equipment company and had become very successful. He had a good salary and a share of the profits. Both were addicted to cocaine.

Although friends, the two played different roles at the Manor. Robert had a firm and unshakable conviction that he was better than other people. Some of this sense of superiority was related to the fact that he came from the richest family in a small town. He liked money and was proud of having it. One day in our room he taught me how to make money at the Manor.

"It's easy," he said. "Everybody smokes. Have your wife buy cartons. Get various brands. Then sell the packs at the same price as the cigarette machines. I made thirty bucks during my first week here."

"But there is nothing to buy here," I observed. "The only vending machines are the cigarette machines and the washing machines in the laundry. There are only so many loads of laundry one person can do." He dismissed me as someone who just didn't get it. He was going somewhere in life. I'd been somewhere and come back. We would never reach each other across that divide.

Robert's friend Rollo was the informal leader of the Barracudas. Rollo was good looking and personable. These qualities had moved him quickly up the ladder in sporting goods and had made him even more success-ful as a cocaine dealer. At the age of twenty-two he owned a nice house, two expensive cars, and half of a restaurant. Although his salary from the sporting goods company was respectable, most of his possessions were a result of his cocaine business. Of all the people at the Manor, getting straight would cost him the most money.

Rollo had a kid-in-a-candy-store attitude about all that had happened to him. He had been born into a rich family, and armed with no more than a high school diploma, had made money at everything he tried. In his early twenties he already had the kind of things people work for decades to get. At times he felt guilty about it. When his employer discovered his addiction, rather than dumping him, the company wrote a check for treatment. He showed up for work one morning and spent that night in a bed at the Manor. Like everyone else at the Manor, I liked Rollo, but doubted he would get sober any time soon.

"Rollo, why do you even want to stop using?" I asked him. "Drugs seem like they've been good to you."

"I'm out of a good job if I don't," he said.

"No one ever quit using for a job."

"I want to stop being scared."

"What are you so scared of?"

"At home I'm afraid of everything. I'm afraid of

phone calls. I'm afraid of knocks on the door. I have money, but never enough to pay the mortgage, the phone bill, and all the others who need to be paid. In my house I can hear a clunk when the mailman drops the mail in the slot. Just the sound of it makes my stomach hurt. I'm scared of mail.

"When you're dealing you have to keep your friends high all the time. You can't be angry at anyone and you can't leave them alone. If you get mad at somebody they go to the cops. If you leave them alone in your house they rip you off and then go to the cops. I want things to be like they are here, where people can't get to you and you don't get mail."

"Who's taking care of your house now?" I asked.

"My parents," he said, "They got everyone out and locked it up."

"Your buddies will be back as soon as you go home."

"Not for long if I can't get them high."

Robert and Rollo were victims. Robert was besieged by a world of people who just didn't get it. Rollo was swept up in a life that wasn't supposed to be his. Robert was a victim of his enemies. Rollo was a victim of his friends.

I felt bad for both of them. Being a victim is one of the most powerful and satisfying feelings in the world. In certain respects I had lived on it for years. Only age and experience can teach a person the pointlessness of it all. Neither of them had the age or the experience. Neither had been hurt enough.

While the basketball game played on television I

rehearsed what I wanted to say to Isol that afternoon. I was changing. I needed to tell her without frightening her. Our separation from each other was difficult enough. The fact that I was becoming a different person wasn't going to make it any easier.

Isol arrive promptly at one o'clock. She was loaded down with supplies, and one of the staff went through the goods at the front door. She carried legal pads, pens, cigarettes, foot spray, golf balls, and my pitching wedge. Communal showers had given me a case of athlete's foot. Despite the affliction, the front desk guard confiscated the foot spray as a threat to my sobriety. The pitching wedge and the remainder of the supplies made it through.

Isol was accompanied by Smugger, one of the Lemmings. Seeing him made me feel ashamed of being where I was. For the Lemmings drinking was a matter of pride. I felt like I'd let them all down.

I stashed my supplies and the three of us went into the dining room for coffee. Conversation was strained. Nothing ever happened at the Manor that I could talk about to outsiders. Nothing ever happened at Taps that anyone cared about. We talked sports and politics.

Smugger escaped after about an hour so that Isol and I could be alone. The two of us took coffees out on the lawn where we could smoke.

The Manor lawn that day had the look of an impressionist painting. Couples strolled across the grass. Groups of children played in the open areas while parents lounged in the shade of the pines. Stevie talked with her husband and children at one of the picnic tables. Daniel was walking the grounds with his parents, always talking. Isol and I spread a blanket in the sun.

"Laura and I cleaned the apartment," Isol said. Laura was her younger sister. "We washed the walls and floors. We shampooed the carpets. We started Friday and worked until midnight last night. Everything is clean for you now."

"That's great," I said.

"I haven't had a drink all week. I had a beer with Smugger after I saw you last Sunday and I haven't had one since."

"You don't have to do that," I said.

"I want to quit with you. If I go to Taps I just think about you."

"I have something to tell you," I said. She turned away.

"I knew it," she said. "I knew this was coming. You're not coming home to me."

"It's not that, Isol," I said. "I want to say I'm sorry. Everything that happened to us was my fault. I've always known it. I ruined both of our lives. I didn't mean to or want to, but I did it. I was selfish. All I could think about was me, and I destroyed everything. I love you. I don't want you to leave me." I couldn't speak for a moment. I took deep breaths and let my tears dry. "Someone once told me," I said, "that a block of stone contains all the sculptures that man can ever produce. It takes the artist to free them from the stone. When I was younger I had in mind to sculpt myself out of the days in front of me. I planned to carve a person who owned nice things and had a comfortable home to rest in at the end of the day. I was going to be a person who was liked and respected. Most of all, I was going to sculpt a person with values, a person whose principles would always be there, even if the possessions and respect never arrived.

"That vision never changed and each morning when I got up I tried to create that person. But every time I looked at what I'd made I'd see something completely different from what I had envisioned. What I sculpted always turned out hideous. I met you and I hoped that with you at my side my art would be better, my hands more sure, my eye more discerning. You stayed with me, put your life in my hands, and I tried to sculpt for both of us. But I couldn't do it. My art was always ugly."

I put my hands on her shoulder and looked into her eyes. "I lost everything for us, Isol. I've ruined my own life and taken you with me. It's all been my fault. I can live with what I've done to myself, but what I did to you is tearing me up inside. I love you with all my heart, but I'm poison to you. I can only make ugly things. I can't make a life for us, and need you to know that you aren't to blame.

"I need to do one more selfish thing. I am going to stop drinking. I'm going to do it for good and for me. I can't do it because I'm sorry, or because I screwed up. I can't do it for you or anyone else. I am going to do it so save my own life."

"Will you still love me?" she asked.

"I'm sober now, and I love you more than I've ever

loved anything. You are all I have left. I've ruined everything else. Things will be different. I don't know what being sober will be like. I don't remember it. I don't know what our life together will be like, but I am going to do it without alcohol."

We hugged for a few minutes, and we cried.

"Knock that off," Stevie yelled. "No sex on the lawn." She and her husband came over. I introduced Isol and the four of us chatted. Stevie and Isol got along well. The bell rang soon after, and visitors had to go. I said my good-bys and stood on the lawn watching until her car pulled out of the parking lot. I'd promised to stop drinking. Next, I had to figure out how to do it.

12

Step two asked that I come to believe that a power greater than myself can restore me to sanity. Step two and step three were the ones I dreaded. They were the God steps.

I had arrived at the Manor a confirmed atheist. I'd been an atheist since high school where I once studied the Bible for the sole purpose of being able to harass Christians with the book's scientific absurdities. I wasn't agnostic. I was atheist. I believed in a world without God. Furthermore, my atheism wasn't based on scientific doubt; it was atheism as a matter of faith. Step two only asked me to believe in a "power greater than myself," however, when I read that phrase I read God.

When the Big Book uses the word God, which it does a lot, the word is followed by the italicized phrase *as you understand him.* This italicized postscript is supposed to avoid sectarianism and open the AA program to people of all religious beliefs. I wasn't impressed by the show of open-mindedness. A "power greater than myself" either meant a large man named Bubba or it meant God. I didn't know anyone named Bubba.

Despite the God problem, I was determined to proceed with the program. The idea of being powerless over alcohol had taken hold of me. Unless I came up with something outside of self, I would be back to will power, and will power was not my friend.

The first thing I did was take a poll of the patients.

Some of the patients were Christians or had at least come from religious backgrounds. These patients tended to believe in a higher power that was a run-of-the-mill, omnipotent, heaven-and-earth creator. Church and wine being closely related, the believers in this kind of God were often winos. The cocaine addicts didn't go to church but usually believed in God. Robert explained it to me. "When you shoot up and the stuff is stronger than you expected, you promise God that if he lets you live through this one you'll give the stuff up forever. If you live, you thank God you still have enough left to do it again."

Daniel found his spiritual guidance in the Far East. His guru had grown up in Mill Valley, California, and his higher power resided in everything from the molecular structure of matter to old Jeopardy reruns. His God asked him to do yoga every morning before breakfast. The idea of physical activity before breakfast convinced me that Daniel's higher power was not for me.

Our C.A., Pixie Patty, had a chicken for a higher power. As a child she had been allergic to fur, so she kept a chicken as a pet. Her chicken died and went to heaven so it could guide her spiritual life. My poll didn't help me find a higher power that could be personal to me, however the chicken idea was briefly attractive.

I ended up taking the easy way out of step two. I accepted the people at the Manor as my higher power. This was presented as an option for atheists and the spiritually bankrupt. Instead of finding God we could take our direction from other recovering addicts. The theory was that we patients, through common experience in addiction and recovery, had molded ourselves into something stronger than the sum of our members. The strength of the group would be my higher power. God, for me would stand for "group of drunks." Drunks understood me. Drunks didn't preach to me or patronize me. Drunks didn't judge me or send me a bill. I came to believe that if I listened to these drunks, I would stay sober. It worked temporarily.

I turned in my step two paperwork and got predictable nods from Wayne. I had invented a higher power out of the addicts at the Manor, the energy of the universe, and the collective consciousness of all addicted people. I thought it was a great higher power. Wayne accepted it as good enough for government work and passed me on to step three.

To help us manage the steps, the staff met with us every afternoon from four to five o'clock for step study. In step study we took turns reading aloud from the book, *Twelve Steps and Twelve Traditions*, and then had short discussions about the reading. By the time step study started we were tired from exercise and hungry for dinner, so the hour was not normally productive. We spent a lot of time in step study talking about living in sobriety one day at a time. In truth, no one knows better than an alcoholic how to live one day at a time. When I was drunk there was no past or future. What mattered was enough booze to keep me drunk until bedtime. With a can of beer and a mouth full of lies, tomorrow never had to come. I knew one day at a time very well, and had no difficulty believing that getting sober was the same way.

In step study we also talked about ways of using the steps to change a lot more than drinking. No one wanted to leave the Manor only to spend eight hours a day in a bar sipping orange juice while all his friends got blasted. No one wanted to continue the lies, fear, and shame that haunt the user. Sobriety had to mean more than just life without liquor.

Prior to coming to the Manor, we spent most of our time getting ready to use, using, and feeling guilty about using. I, for example, knew only two people who didn't drink and I didn't like either one of them. My social life took place in taverns. A round of golf started with a beer and ended with a six pack. Life without drugs left huge blank spaces in my daily existence— extra hours in my day with nothing to fill them. Everyone at the Manor had a similar problem: what to do with the time. Pixie Patty once told me, "We don't ask much here. We ask only that you completely change your life." Much of the change would have to be in what we did with the hours of the day.

Step three mentions God by name. It required me to turn my life and will over to "God, *as I understood him.*" The God stuff was not leaving me alone.

I should have been better prepared for the barrage of God. I was reasonably well read in theology and the history of religion, but my expertise was academic. I accepted that some people had deeply spiritual sensations and that spiritual changes had caused many people to drastically change their behaviors. Yet, at a gut level, I felt that anyone who claimed to have personally experienced God was crazy, lying, or mistaken.

Denying the existence of an otherworldly omnipotent God is easy. Denying the value of faith takes creativity. I used several handy arguments for disbelieving the experiences of the faithful. First, I dismissed the liars and the loons as nothing more than liars and loons. I figured TV preachers and anyone else who made a living from religion was a liar and a greedy liar at that. I knew about lying and I knew about greed. I dismissed anyone who stood on the street giving away copies of the Watchtower as a loon because no respectable God would require a person to do such embarrassing things. Having dealt with the liars and loons, I turned my attention to the mistaken.

Those who weren't loons and had no reason to lie, I surmised, had simply made an error. They were honest people who had been fooled into believing something that was not true. Explaining how reasonable people have been deceived into believing they have a relationship with God is different than picking on the liars and loons. I could not fairly group Tolstoy, C.S. Lewis, and Mother Theresa with those who had seen Big Foot or been abducted by UFOs. Explaining away the religious experiences of honest and intelligent believers required more of me than intellectual contempt, but I had never afraid of challenges.

One method I had used for rejecting the worth of faith was to attribute the spiritual experience to an organic cause. This is an easy approach for those of us with a scientific or skeptical nature. I could deflect attention from the fact and value of another's spiritual experience by connecting it to a natural cause. If the cause of a spiritual feeling was something mundane, such as an excess of hormones or a bad burrito, all the better, for if the cause is silly, so must be the effect. By associating the spiritual experience with natural forces other than God, I tarred the effect with values connected to the cause. This intellectual slight-of-hand was clever, but ultimately dishonest, and part of what I was trying to do was reduce my dishonesty.

The first problem with my analysis was that the logical problems surrounding cause and effect are just as knotty as those that surround God. The second problem was that the cause of a religious or spiritual experience is probably irrelevant. The proper yardstick is the value of the experience to the person and ultimately to society. Spiritual changes were enabling people to stop drinking, even after years of dehabilitating alcoholism. The spiritual changes made those same people tend to believe in God. The belief and the behavioral changes went hand in hand. It didn't really matter whether the change within was ordained by God or triggered by the bad burrito, the effect was real, and, for the person transformed, God was real. Finding a mundane antecedent for what happened could not change the event. In a similar sense, I might explain the physics of a sunset, but my explanation cannot diminish its beauty.

An easier method I'd used to dismiss the accomplishments of faith was to find the evidence lacking. Evidence of transformation through spiritual change is anecdotal; it comes only from the testimony of the person changed. "Anecdotal evidence" is a phrase from the medical field used to discount things that have not been statistically demonstrated according to whatever methodology happens to be popular at the time the issue arises. For me, anything that did not fit into test groups, mathematical formulas, and success rates got shoved into the anecdotal bin with all the other random unexplained occurrences that the universe springs upon us. Spiritual rearrangements were the kind of things that happened to Kentucky coal miners in revival meetings, not the kind of things that happened to me.

At another level my difficulty with faith also had to do with the lists of feelings that Wayne made me write. I seldom had feelings, as far as I could tell, and to the extent that I did, I believed that the only proper feelings for a man were pride, anger, and lust. The others, particularly those surrounding spirituality, were women's feelings. Objects, whether they be physical, like the coffee table in my living room, or conceptual, like *pi*, were real. Objects were verifiable because they existed in the minds of other people exactly the way they existed in mine. When enough people perceive a thing the same way it becomes a fact. I believed in facts.

Feelings were not facts to me. Some of them approached the level of facts, but most did not. I assumed that most people experienced feelings such as pain, hunger, and fatigue in essentially the same way. However, feelings associated with love, anger or sexuality seemed to vary widely depending upon the individual. The pedophile feels his sexuality quite differently from the nun. Feelings were for the poet, not the scientist. A bottle of beer is real. No amount of poetry or emotionalism can change that.

Both Wayne and I were wrong about feelings. I had them. I'd always had them. I had traded the normal human feelings for the feelings of drunkenness. For a long time it was a trade I made willingly. Then when I no longer wanted to drink—when I wanted the regular feelings back—I couldn't find them. Sober and without them, I felt nothing.

Feelings may not be facts, but people respond to feelings as if they are. A hungry person eats. A new mother clings to her child. A man works overtime for the pride and the feeling of success. Addicts use drugs to feel good. When I was afraid, alcohol dulled the fear. When I was happy alcohol made me happier. When I was suicidal, alcohol took me into the zone. Feelings, not objects, fill the hours of my life. An object has purpose and value to me only to the extent that it causes me to feel a certain way. We choose our cars, houses, and careers based upon how they make us feel. Our Darwinian drive for self-preservation acts through feelings. We eat to feel good. We sleep to renew our strength. We make love for the way it makes us feel. Survival is the result, but not the goal. By all accounts feeling God, sensing the divine in our personal lives, is one of the most satisfying feelings a person can experience. It was, however, among the many feelings that I had yet to write down in my notebook.

I think I was too proud for God. As a drunk, even a sober drunk, I could lay in the gutter and look with disdain on the world. Admitting value in spiritual experiences threatened my life long sense of superiority. Accepting God meant I had been dead wrong about important things for twenty years. It meant I had been deceived. It meant that other people had experienced something that I hadn't, something that no amount of money or education could replace. Set against the Big Book my arguments against faith did not seem as well reasoned as they once had been. Other people had found sobriety through faith. I wanted sobriety. I even wanted faith. But no person can will himself to believe. It must just come. Faith had not come to me, and I could not will myself to have it.

I fantasized about God. I didn't need much for a God. I didn't care if God created the heaven and the earth. I didn't care if God was Christian, Moslem or Hindu. All I wanted was a God who could take away my desire to drink. I wanted one that would take away my guilt and my fear. Those were the only miracles I needed.

One night in the basement lounge, after reading the Big Book, I prayed. Prayer is a difficult thing for an atheist. It is doubly difficult for an atheist who has ridiculed and bad-mouthed God for more than twenty years. For me, asking help from God was humiliating.

I said my prayer softly, yet aloud. My voice seemed small in the empty basement lounge. I stopped and checked the hall outside to make sure I wouldn't be overheard and then started again. In my first prayer I couldn't summon the nerve to ask for anything. I could dial the number but I couldn't yet ask for help. I asked God to tell me what to do and promised that if he did, I would do my best to do it. I told him my best wasn't all that good, but going it alone hadn't turned out well for me. I said "Amen" when it was over. No walls came tumbling down. No trumpets played. Nothing happened.

13

"The bitch," Stevie said. She slammed the smoking room door behind her and paced across the room. "She took my perfume, nail polish, mouthwash and body lotion. All threats to my goddamn sobriety."

Stevie's less-than-kind words were for Tess, a tall masculine looking woman who was the most experienced of the counselors and also the most severe. She was a heroin addict who had beome, in sobriety, the terror of the Manor. She seldom smiled, and when she did it was usually at someone else's expense. I disliked her, as did most of the patients. The other counselors and the C.A.s were afraid of her.

Tess had found the cosmetics that Stevie's husband had smuggled to her during the Sunday visit. In theory, they were confiscated because they contained alcohol or traces of other psychoactive drugs. One of the stories at the Manor was about a patient who drank nail polish remover in an attempt to get high. Most of the staff overlooked minor violations when it came to cosmetics. Tess enforced the rule because it was the rule, and she enjoyed it.

Since coming to the Manor I had taken the path of least resistance and simply avoided Tess. Stevie was constitutionally incapable of doing so. Rules bothered Stevie. Silly rules drove her crazy.

The morning Stevie lost her make-up was also the day of the outing. Every Thursday, patients with enough seniority were allowed outside the Manor for recreation. My name was on the list of lucky patients on the blackboard when I arrived for morning meditation. The board said that Tess was to be our driver and chaperon.

As I read the thought for the day Stevie glared across the room at Tess. At the end of meditation Tess told those of us on the outing list that we would either be going to Multnomah Falls or a bowling alley. Multnomah Falls is a park and waterfall a few miles outside of Portland. Bowling is the same everywhere.

"Bowling," Stevie snapped. Tess didn't respond in the slightest. "Bowling," Stevie repeated.

After meditation we went to the dining room to watch the second half of *The Days of Wine and Roses* on video. I liked the movie. I was watching it with one eye and drawing pictures with the other when Stevie sidled up to my chair.

"Do you want bowling or Multnomah Falls?" she asked.

"I don't care," I told her.

"Yeah you do. You want bowling."

"Okay," I said, "I want bowling."

"So, can I put you down for bowling?"

"Sure, do I need to sign a petition?"

"No. I just want to be able to tell Tess that most people want to go bowling."

"Well, Include me." I didn't care where we went, but I liked Stevie, and if she liked bowling, that was fine with me. I certainly didn't want to stand in her way if she was on a mission.

Between the movie and the start of group, Stevie canvassed the smoking room making notes of who was a bowler and who wanted to commune with nature. It turned out that despite Stevie's cajoling only slightly more than half of the people scheduled for the outing favored the bowling alley. In the break before lunch Stevie went to find Tess and present the results of her poll.

"Are you a bowling man, or a Multnomah Falls man?" I asked Daniel.

"Multnomah Falls," he said. "Can I have one of your cigarettes?" Daniel was constantly quitting smoking. This week he had thrown away the carton his parents brought him and was surviving on the generosity of others until the next visiting day.

"Why the nature walk instead of the lanes?" I asked.

"Oh, I wouldn't mind bowling," he said, "but on the outside I seldom play games with rules. I prefer pure play to the structure of games."

"Well, people play when they play games," I pointed out.

"True. Games are a part of play, a subset if you like. Games have rules. They are precisely limited in time and space, like a stint here at the Manor. A chess match takes place on sixty-four squares, and for the pros, a precise amount of time is allowed for each game. Football lasts exactly an hour on a grass rectangle."

"A baseball game could theoretically last forever," I interjected, "if the score stayed a tie."

"Only in theory," Daniel said. "Sooner or later the players would exercise the option of just quitting and going home. The aborted game would then be remembered as unsatisfying to everyone because it did not end according to the rules. However, if you and I went out on the baseball field to play Frisbee, the activity could easily stray off the field and up into the stands without any violation of the rules. We could play until one of us got tired and then stop without any sense of incompleteness. Play is over when it's over, not at the sound of the bell, or for that matter, upon graduation."

"I get bored without rules though," I told him. "I can go to the golf course and hit balls on the driving range, but it's boring. No matter how much I need the practice, I want to get out on the course and start counting strokes."

"It is a matter of temperament," Daniel said. "When I see a golf course, I get the urge to explore it with a picnic lunch. I'm fascinated by the combination of nature and architecture. I'd like to wade in the streams and make castles in the sand traps."

"If a flying golf ball didn't kill you an angry golfer would," I told him.

"Exactly. The golfer gets pleasure from striving against the golf course. He pits his strength, ability, and cleverness against the course. He takes pride in the fact that, no matter how bad his score, he gave it his best shot. With my picnic basket in hand I don't strive against the course, I commune with it. I put a blanket in the sun and become a part of the surroundings. That makes me happy. The golfer and the picnic basket cannot coexist. Consequently, no matter how much I'd like to, I do not play Frisbee or have picnics on golf courses."

"Some golfers enjoy Frisbee, and vise versa," I suggested.

"Absolutely. Everyone likes recreation. Some people live for it. Sometimes it is structured into games and sometimes not, but you can't play and play games at the same time. No one plays Frisbee while pulling clubs down the fairway."

"So how about the game of one-upmanship that Stevie is playing with Tess?" I asked.

"I suspect they are both deadly serious," he said. "Whatever it is, it is not recreation."

"But isn't Stevie playing a little Frisbee on Tess's golf course?"

"That's where the fun ends."

"So what happens next, professor?"

"I don't know," he said. "Life, I suppose."

Life went on at lunch. Tess had accepted the results of Stevie's poll with pointed indifference. Tess did not eat lunch with us and Stevie was sulking. We were finishing our meal when Tess came in and announced, "All those going on the outing have to be at the van at twelve thirty sharp. We're going to Multnomah Falls." The die was cast.

"Most of us want to go bowling," Stevie declared.

"Don't be late," Tess said.

"What about bowling?" Stevie demanded.

"Jack can't go bowling. His rib injury won't allow it."

Stevie was stuck. Indian Jack hardly ever said or did anything. Stevie, I'm sure, had never considered polling him. Yet, here he was the trump card on Stevie's lead.

"He could watch," Stevie suggested meekly. The suggestion was realistic in that watching was what Jack seemed to do most of the time, however, it lacked any moral base. Democracy was no match for sympathy. We were headed for Multnomah Falls.

I was the first one to show up at the van. I stood on the sunny side of the vehicle and lit a cigarette. The spring air was cool, but my skin warmed quickly in the sun. I hadn't been there long when Jack showed up. He leaned against the van a few feet from where I stood.

"How's it going Jack?" I asked.

"My ribs hurt a lot today," he said. "They shouldn't make me go."

"Who said you have to go?" I asked, already knowing the answer.

"The tall lady said so." Tess was the counselor assigned to him, yet he could only refer to her as the tall lady.

Big John showed up next. He was followed by Robert and Rollo. Stevie and her roommate, Carol, were the last to arrive. The mood of the group turned jovial in the sunshine. Even Stevie cheered up a bit as we joked and contemplated the outing. Tess showed up a fashionable ten minutes late and we climbed into the van.

Anticipation ran high, even though most everyone had seen Multnomah Falls many times before. The excitement rose, not because of the eventual destination, but because before leaving the city we would all be permitted a few precious minutes inside a convenience store. For the remainder of the afternoon we could possess all the sugar and caffeine a person could carry. The stop at the store before outings was a Manor tradition.

In the parking lot of the store, the engine was hardly off when we burst out of the side doors and dashed toward the goodies inside. Showing amazing nimbleness for his size and age, Big John led the pack like an escaping Santa Claus pursued by elves. Once inside we broke into two groups. One went for candy and the other headed for carbonated beverages. In the candy aisle Robert and Rollo scared away two pre-teen boys and started cramming sugar into their pockets. Those who'd gone to the soda machine apportioned soda and ice into seventy-two ounce mega-cups. I bought several Reese's peanut butter cups, a bag of peanuts, sunflower seeds, and a seventy-two ounce Mountain Dew. Mountain Dew was reputed among the patients to have more sugar and caffeine than any other soda.

The sugar and caffeine high that followed took me back to my early days of drugs. I felt warm when it was cold outside. The people in the van were the best friends I'd ever known. Big John, riding shotgun with Tess, found an oldie-goldie station and we sang along with the radio as the van rumbled along the wide Columbia River toward the Multnomah Falls. I, like most people, never tire of watching water flow down-hill. We parked in a huge parking lot next to the free-way and the inmates made for the water. Tess tried briefly to keep the group together, but quickly accepted that it wasn't going to happen.

Once at the visitor's center, everyone felt free to move about at will. Robert and Rollo set off on the steep path to the top of the falls. Stevie and her roommate, Carol, determined not to enjoy the trip, settled down on a park service bench and smoked cigarettes. Big John and I went to explore the souvenir shop. Life at the Manor had no commerce. John and I wanted to go where money changed hands.

The souvenir shop had a predictable collection of postcards, key chains, and Oregon memorabilia. The theme of the shop was wood. Oregon has a lot of wood. The shop sold wooden boxes, games, carvings, cooking utensils, and gags. I shopped for Isol, wanting to buy her something for supporting me. My wallet though was nearly empty, so any gift would have to be symbolic. After long consideration I bought a cedar sachet carved in the shape of an egg. I didn't know what it symbolized, but it was pleasing to hold.

At the entrance to the store a flight of stairs led to an upstairs bar. I went outside and looked up at three large windows behind which people sat nursing drinks and watching the waterfall. A cold wind whipped down the gorge, and those of us outside kept our hands buried in our coat pockets. I knew the people in the bar were warm, and regretted that we couldn't all go up there and celebrate with a drink.

As I stood outside Tess walked slowly by with Jack who was hunched over holding his ribs. I wondered what kind of relationship they had. It had to be quite different from my relationship with Wayne. To him, she was just one of the white people. I could not understand what he was to her.

Stevie and Carol were still smoking on the bench when Tess passed. Stevie glared at Tess. Tess noticed, but didn't look as the roommates made a show of not having fun. I walked up the path to the spot where the falling water hit the pool at the bottom. Daniel and Big John were standing at the railing watching. I joined them in the mist and stared silently at the water.

After an hour or so at the falls, Tess made the rounds directing everyone back to the van. Rather than taking the freeway back to town, we took the winding back roads that criss-cross the Oregon side of the gorge. The two-lane highway snaked through the rain forest. Ferns covered the forest floor and smaller waterfalls appeared from the side of the mountain every few hundred yards. I felt primeval forces at work and had a sense that were the van to stop for any period of time it would be quickly overgrown and swallowed up by the damp greenery.

Reaching a flat area, Tess pulled the van into the parking lot of a scenic viewpoint overlooking the Columbia Gorge. We climbed out into the cold gorge wind and walked toward a small stone wall that prevented tourists from plunging off the edge of the cliff. I shivered in the cold. From the wall we could see in both directions to where the Columbia disappeared into the horizon. Mount Saint Helens, its top having blown off in a volcanic explosion while I was in law school, stood majestically snow-capped in the distance. A container ship filled with lumber appeared motionless as it made its way toward the ocean. I felt the peculiar sense of smallness, powerlessness if you will, that comes from watching the massiveness of nature at work.

When we returned to the van I took a seat next to Stevie. She and Carol had remained in the van, citing the cold wind and a lack of interest in looking at any more water. They had maintained the silent protest to the bitter end.

Back in the warm van, I felt sleepy. The sugar and caffeine was wearing off. I closed my eyes and let myself sway with the motion of the van as it moved. Everyone was quiet. Several of us slept.

At one point I opened my eyes. Everyone except Stevie was dosing or gazing out windows. Stevie was staring at Tess.

"How are you doing on your steps?" I asked her.

"I'm doing okay," she said. "I should be able to turn in the paperwork for step three in a couple of days."

"If you don't mind my asking," I said, "what are you doing with the God stuff."

"I've always believed in God," she said, "or at least that the universe is not an accident."

"Your God created the universe?"

"Yeah, sort of. I don't really accept that God sits around meddling much in affairs here in Portland."

"He takes the hands off approach?" I asked.

"She, if you don't mind," Stevie said. "She helps those who help themselves. She endowed me with the ability to get what I want. I'm sure of that. When I'm loaded I don't even know what I want."

"What do you want now?" I asked.

"I want to humiliate Tess the way she did to me. And, I want to do it sober."

"That's not very Christian," I said.

"I'm not a Christian."

"Pouting is going about it the wrong way."

"How should I go about it?"

"I have an idea," I said. "I'll show you tomorrow."

14

Step four was the big one. It required me to make "a searching and fearless moral inventory" of myself. Step four was so big we took our directions from Sky Pilot, the Manor clergyman. The step was a constant topic of conversation among the patients. Those who hadn't gotten it dreaded it. Those who were doing it anguished over it and worried about whether their jottings were adequately hidden when they weren't writing.

I turned in my third step work, and Wayne passed me on with another series of grunts and nods. I didn't tell him about my attempt at prayer in the basement. I didn't regret the prayer; I just didn't want anyone to know about it.

Wayne asked again how I thought I was doing. Once again, I didn't know how to answer. "You look better," he said. That was something. I turned in my latest drawings. He always liked the drawings, and I had the feeling they might show up in some academic tome on the psychology of addiction. After passing me on step three, Wayne told me to meet with Sky Pilot to receive my fourth step.

I'd been to see Sky Pilot when I first arrived at the Manor so he could record my religious leanings. The Manor allowed certain variations on the house rules to accommodate a person's religious views. A synagogue was available in case the Manor ever got a Jew. All other denominations were permitted to attend Sunday services at a nearby Lutheran Church. Most of the patients came in without any religious leanings. I came in an atheist. My first meeting with Sky Pilot had been short. The second was more interesting.

Sky Pilot's office was on the first floor close to administration. He was a tall white-haired man in his early sixties. His small book-lined office had a scholarly look to it. On his desk was a picture of his young wife. When I arrived for my appointment he invited me into a comfortable overstuffed chair.

He introduced himself with a thumbnail sketch of his life. The autobiography was designed, I imagine, to put me at ease with him as a spiritual advisor. Ministering was a second career for him. After twenty years he'd become dissatisfied with selling widgets, buried one wife, married a new young one, and had never been addicted to anything. I knew everything he would say from having listened to patients who had listened to him before me.

Sky Pilot tried to make a connection with me based upon education. He had a PHD in divinity. I had a JD in law. He was quietly smug about his degrees and the books on his shelves. I threw books away when I finished them and considered graduate degrees evidence of a person's tolerance for pretentious horseshit. We both had education, but we differed about its value.

"Have you experienced any changes in your views regarding a creator?" he asked.

"No," I said. I was not about to tell him about the prayer. I was terrified that if he saw a crack in my resolve he would start hounding me to leap into Lutheranism.

Sky Pilot then attempted to make a case for God.

In a friendly bumbling sort of way he presented the if-there's-a-watch-there-must-be-a-watchmaker theory. The argument goes as follows: if one sees a beautiful painting there must have been a great artist at work. For there to be a fine watch there has to have been a watchmaker. Thus, if there is beauty and order in the natural world, there had to be a creator. The creator, lo and behold, is God. People who attempt this sort of reasoning on a nonbeliever should remember the old adage: "Never try to teach a pig to sing, it's a waste of time and it annoys the pig." I was the pig, and I was annoyed.

As far as I was concerned, the value, beauty, and mystery of a watch, a painting, or the universe was in the thing itself. Watchmakers and painters tend to be a disreputable lot, folks trying to grub out a living like the rest of us, often alcoholic. Why should those who create universes be any different? According to Sky Pilot's logic, God could be an idiot savant living in a cosmic asylum. Or worse, he could have been a Hemingway type who did his best work and then killed himself. Where would that leave us? I didn't care about the origin of watches, paintings, or the wonders of nature. I needed a personal God who could take away my obsession with alcohol.

I wanted to tell Sky Pilot that he was doing it all wrong. I wanted to be convinced about God and wanted him to tell me about faith. Faith, I wanted him to say, is believing in something even though it has not been, and cannot ever be, proven true. It is being an optimist when all evidence supports pessimism. The scientist collects data in his laboratory to discover immutable laws of nature. If he did not accept on faith the proposition that the laws of nature remain the same from day to day, there would be no point to his labors. The mountain climber in mortal danger who believes that he can leap the crevasse to safety has better odds of making it out alive than the climber who can't believe. I wanted him to explain to me that without faith there is paralysis and failure; with faith there is action, and with action we have a chance to make what we believe come true. The man who accepts only proven facts is always the last one through the door. He is by necessity a follower. Faith in God's help, I wanted him to tell me, was my door to sanity—that my life depended on it.

I thought that if he had told it to me my way, I might have believed him. But he didn't. I chalked it up as another of the failures of organized religion.

Getting nowhere on the spiritual front, Sky Pilot moved on to the fourth step. He explained that I was to evaluate my life in moral terms. He gave me a crudely stapled booklet containing a general outline of what I was to do. It started with the misdemeanors: sloth, envy, pride, gluttony and the like. It worked from there to felonies: adultery, theft and murder. I was to explain in detail what part in my life each of these sins had played. I understood the concept.

I noticed that the printing in my booklet was blurry from having been photocopied and rephotocopied many times. The original had come from a publisher in central California. I thought to myself that the publisher might have profited more from the publication if he'd included copyright infringement in the list of sins.

The booklet emphasized sin. The Big Book emphasized character defects and resentments. The booklet used religious terms; the Big Book used psychological ones. I didn't care. Lying may be a character defect or a sin. Self centeredness may be ego or pride. The result is the same. The liar lives in fear of the truth. The egoist is unable to like himself. Sinners suffer on earth the guilt, fear, and anger that sin produces. Those with character defects suffer the same. Fortunately, step four didn't require me to do anything about my sins and character defects. It asked only that I sort them out and write them down.

No one had gotten to the Manor without a bucket full of failures. I brought lost jobs, broken promises, and trust betrayed, all served up on a platter of everyday lies. During the fourth step I was asked to digest it all into a single document.

Every person has a secret he intends to take to his grave. Alcoholics have lots of them. I had a decade full, and my container of the unrevealable was overflowing. That evening I took four new legal pads and put them on the desk in my room with a new pen. I gazed at the workplace I had created, and not wanting to disturb its perfect structure, went to the smoking room for a cigarette. A pile of blank paper was a good start.

In the smoking room Big John and Stevie were playing competitive solitaire.

"I got step four today," I told them.

"How is Sky Pilot?" Stevie asked, "Still feeling

guilty?"

"He's fine," I told her.

"You should do your step four with illustrations," Big John suggested. "Do it comic book style."

"I could title it 'The Adventures of Drunkman,'" I said.

" . . . and his faithful companion Cokeboy," Big John added.

Stevie said, "Wayne asked me to check your fourth step for spelling and grammar. Just give me the pages as you write."

"Yeah," I said, "in your dreams."

"Come on," she cajoled, "you've got nothing to hide, do you?"

"Right, I'm really a living saint. I was on my way to help orphans and got locked up here by accident. I just now remembered that. I better go now so I can get back to my saintly duties."

"John," Stevie said, "Give this man some advice. You're a veteran of treatment centers. You must have done step four a few times."

"Only once before this," John said. "The army sent me to treatment the first time. They gave me barbiturates so I wouldn't drink. It worked. Taking barbiturates, and heroin for that matter, always causes me to cut back on my drinking. The second treatment was part of a parole. There I got aversion treatment. They gave me Antabuse and made me drink. Drink and puke. Drink and puke. That program taught me that it was better to be drunk and sick than not be drunk at all.

"In my last stint I got the steps. I did steps one

through eight. When I got out I started with step nine and AA. I stayed sober for three and a half years. I was laid off for a few weeks at one point and one day I just up and got drunk. I don't know why. I guess I wanted one more drunk. That drunk lasted eleven months and ended me up here."

"How can you be serious about it when it didn't work last time?" I asked.

"It did work last time," he said. "Three and a half years was the longest I'd ever been straight in my life. If I quit for life this time, that's great. If I get another three years out of it, that's fine too. If I make it through today, it's better than being drunk."

"One day at a time," Stevie chanted without looking up from the cards.

"Well, I don't want my Drunkman adventure to end with a 'to be continued,'" I said.

"Do the steps," John said. "Really do them and go to AA. Go every day when you get out. The people who drink don't do the steps and don't go to meetings. The people who do those things don't drink."

"You went to AA," I said, "and you drank again."

"I quit going," he said. "I got tired of it. I quit going because I'd been sober for three years and didn't need it anymore. I was drunk three months later."

"One day at a time," Stevie repeated.

"Kiss off with the 'one day at a time,'" I said.

"Thank you," she said.

"Are you doing step four, Stevie?" I asked.

"Not yet," she said, "I'm still turning my life and will over to God."

"Well there's no God in step four," I said.

"Being a saint and all, you should have the God stuff down pat."

"No problem," I told her.

Writing step four was dirty and painful. I started it as far back in my life as I could remember: my first lies, my first theft, my earliest envies and resentments. As I wrote about one thing hundreds of others bubbled into consciousness. I was digging in quicksand. The yellow pads filled with words. When a pad was full I shoved it into the bottom of my desk drawer beneath my socks. I wrote about pride, arrogance, cruelty, and betrayal. I wrote about the people I'd hurt, and I wrote about hurting myself.

As I wrote the going got easier. Certain memories made me wince, however, even the worst of them lost power once down on paper. The paper and ink sucked out the terrors the memories held. As I felt relief I wrote harder and dug deeper.

Writing the fourth step took place amid the other activities at the Manor, but once I got going I became engrossed with it, finishing the bulk of it in a intense two day stretch. I never evaluated or even read what I wrote. I didn't draw conclusions or learn any lessons. I simply wrote.

As I look back on my fourth step I remember very little about the writing. The details of doing my first three steps are all clear to me. The fourth is missing. Despite all the drinking that had proceeded my coming to the Manor, the writing of my fourth step was my first blackout.

15

A couple of days after the trip to Multnomah Falls I fulfilled my promise to Stevie. I didn't feel well the morning that I did it, and feeling poorly put me in the mood to cause trouble.

At breakfast I said to Stevie, "Today we play with Tess."

"Okay," she said, "what's up?"

"Soften her up at meditation, and get some bodies to help out during exercise."

"Help with what?"

"A gauntlet."

I don't know why I took up the standard in Stevie's battle with Tess. I had never had a serious run-in with Tess. Maybe I missed being a lawyer—participating in other people's battles without making them my own. More likely, there was no more reason for it than the reasons I had for drinking.

My plan required my one piece of contraband. In a corner of my room my pitching wedge was leaning against the wall. I had a small plastic bucket and five golf balls under my desk. Isol brought them during her second visit and, for reasons unbeknownst to me, they had not been confiscated at the front door.

Someone had screwed up. The golf club was contraband because it could be used as a weapon, and a very effective one at that. Were I to go berserk and decide to massacre a few unruly patients I could do a good bit of damage by applying the blade of the pitching wedge to someone's head.

The golf club caused quite a bit of comment among the patients. Rules required our doors to be open at all times so everyone knew what kind of things other patients owned. Daniel found it irritating that his keys had been confiscated lest he stab someone, yet I was permitted a hunk of metal deadlier than a three-foot length of rebar. Both Cowboy Bob and Pixie Patty had advised me to keep the golf club out of sight. They both emphasized that they weren't concerned about *my* mental stability, but that some other patient might get a hold of it and do serious harm to the Manor or its occupants. They should have worried about me.

Tess led meditation that morning. When she asked for someone to read the daily homily, Stevie answered quickly, "I'll read."

"Are there other volunteers?" Tess asked. Prompted by Stevie's aggressive volunteerism, everyone else stared at the floor. Stevie began reading. She read quickly, without inflection or punctuation, thereby making the meditation nearly incomprehensible. When she was done Tess asked for comment. No one said a word. Sensing group obstinance, Tess ended meditation early and we reconvened in the smoking room for morning gossip.

Just before lunch there was a graduation ceremony for my roommate, Robert. Graduations were held every time a person's insurance ran out. We would gather in one of the ornately furnished first floor rooms. In Robert's case, his wife, parents, and grandparents attended. The patients sat on folding chairs moved in from the dining room while his relatives got the upholstered chairs and couches. Counselors and C.A.s stood in the doorways or against the wall.

The graduation ceremony was governed by Manor tradition. First, Robert's counselor, a retired military man who had nursed his alcoholism in the Navy, gave a short speech about how much Robert had changed since coming to treatment. When finished he gave Robert a coin stamped with the Serenity Prayer and a picture of the Manor. As Robert received the coin we all applauded. Robert said a few words of thanks to the Manor staff and offered a good word to those of us who were staying. We applauded again. To end the affair, family, staff, and patients lined up to give Robert a hug and words of encouragement. When the hugs were over Robert was free to leave.

I disliked the graduations. The Manor was a safe port in the storm for me. Graduations reminded me how temporary it all was, and that the real world waited outside. Insurance companies would only put up with so much nonsense, and the Manor staff did not coddle us from dawn to dusk for free.

Graduations also meant a change in the make-up of the patients. A different drunk would fill Robert's bed in my room. Robert had been a considerate room-mate, and we had patched together an uneasy friend-ship. His leaving reminded me that all the patients who welcomed me to the Manor would leave before I would. Already I was gaining seniority. New people, still in withdrawal, asked me about the rules or the where-abouts of the laundry soap. I didn't like it. I wished I could stop the changes, and we could all stay permanently at the Manor, going from room to room in perpetuity, at the sound of the bell.

After lunch I saw Robert in our room packing his belongings in a duffel bag. "You should take my mattress before someone new comes," he told me. "It's the firmest one."

"I'll do that," I said. Mine was a bag of feathers. He helped me change the mattress from his bed to mine.

"Good luck out there," I said as we shook hands. Our friendship did not extend to anything unmanly.

"I'll be fine," he said. "Come visit me when you get down the coast. I'd like to meet your wife. We could go to dinner or something."

"We'll do that," I said.

"Maybe I'll see you in court."

"Who knows." We shook hands and I left to have a smoke. When the bell sounded, I returned to the room to get my notebook. Robert and his things were gone.

That afternoon, when the bell rang for exercise. I went to my room for the golf club. Someone had piled clean folded sheets and towels on Robert's stripped bed. I picked up my pitching wedge and golf balls and took the basement exit out of the building.

Just beyond the volleyball court lay an unused stretch of grass about the size of a football field. I carried the golf equipment to the farthest corner of the field, safely away from the volleyball but in clear view of the second floor counselor's lounge where Tess took her coffee.

The spring weather was perfect for golf. The club felt heavy and comfortable. I let the club swing loosely in my left hand a few times then took my stance. The wedge bit into the turf, and the feel of the club reminded me of good times. Despite all that happened, there had been good times.

I dropped my five balls in a line on the lawn. When I hit the first ball it popped out of the grass and landed about fifteen yards in front of me. Using the first ball as a target, I hit the other four. The volleyball game had started. A couple of patients were walking the perimeter of the grounds. Pixie Patty was talking to others at a picnic table near the volleyball game. Indian Jack was alone, leaning against a tree a few yards from the table.

I lined up the balls again, and, by increasing my backswing, dropped a ball about twenty yards down the field. The others landed within a reasonable distance of the first. I followed the same procedure to the hedge at the edge of the Manor grounds, then turned around and started hitting balls back toward where I'd started. The C.A.s in the yard paid me no attention. Wayne and another counselor had come out to watch volleyball for a moment then returned to the building. My theory was that nobody would care except Tess. Everything was up to her.

During my third trip down the field, Tess came out the front door on a mission. The walk to my makeshift fairway took her between the volleyball game and the picnic table, allowing her to draw all eyes. I kept hitting balls, trying to keep my swing and demeanor uniform. I didn't turn to face her until she was about ten yards away. She came within a few feet of me before speaking. "You can't play golf here," she said.

"Okay," I answered.

"You can't play golf on Manor grounds."

"Okay," I said again. She stared at me as if expecting me to protest. I put the balls in the bucket and held my club by the shaft to show submission. Tess turned and started toward the building. I followed holding my club.

Stevie had stopped the volleyball game. The players stood in a loose line to the left of the route back to the building. The patients from the picnic table stood on our right. The walkers, Jack and a couple o young guys from the basketball court joined them; the two groups forming a gauntlet through which Tess and I had to pass.

Big John started. "Busted," he boomed. "Golf bum, criminal, degenerate." The people on both sides joined in.

"Reprobate. Pervert."

"Threat to sobriety. Threat to society"

"You make me want to drink."

"Shame."

"I'm gonna relapse, help me."

I hung my head in mock shame. The crowd inched forward on both sides throwing small handfuls of grass at me as I walked behind Tess. No one said a word directly to her.

"You're a disgrace," Stevie yelled, "You need to be protected from yourself. I hope they crucify you."

"Communist," someone yelled.

"Nazi."

"Save the children."

"Save the Pope."

"Save Arnold Palmer."

"Go Blazers." They yelled anything from nonsense to old sports cheers. I savored the sounds. It was the sound of friends. Stevie started a chant, "Save the Manor, No golf. Save the Manor, No golf." The chanters were still going full force when I closed the Manor door behind me.

Tess never turned to look at me. As soon as we were inside the door she walked to the counselor's lounge. I found myself standing alone on the first floor with my club and balls. The plan had gone better than expected. I put the club in my room and went for a smoke. The others joined me later in the smoking room and we had a celebration.

"Her face was perfect," Rollo observed, "Curiosity, then confusion, then irritation. From annoyance to rage in twenty-five yards."

"Did you see that vein in her neck?" John asked, "I do believe her serenity was disturbed."

"She's always disturbed," Stevie said, "It was perfect. No one said a single word to her or against her, not a single word."

"I didn't like the stuff you said about me, though," I told her.

"No one cares about you?" she said, "Tess looked at me. She knew I set her up and she knew why."

"You set her up?" I said.

"Okay, we did it, but she knew why." Stevie flopped into a chair. "Christ, I feel good."

"I must admit," Daniel said, "It an excellent

exercise in group sarcasm."

"Don't start analyzing it, professor. Relish it," Stevie told him.

"I enjoyed it," he said. "It was clever. I even yelled."

"I hope it bugs her for weeks," Stevie said. "I hope she gets so up-tight her hole heals shut."

"Frightening thought," Daniel said.

The gloating continued until the bell rang for step study. We settled down, gathered our Twelve Step books and reconvened in the meditation room. Pixie Patty led the group. As the patients took turns reading about step three I closed my eyes. I felt sleepy.

Wayne's voice startled me from a reverie of home. He asked me to see him outside. The group was silent for a moment as I stepped outside the room. He motioned me away from the open door so our conversation wouldn't be heard. He was nervous and embarrassed. "I'm sorry," he said, "I have to confiscate your golf club."

I laughed. I couldn't help it. "That's fine, Wayne. Don't worry about it," I said. "It's up in my room. Just go get it. You know my door is always open for you."

"Thanks," he said. I rejoined the patients for the rest of step study. When I went into my room before dinner the club was gone.

That evening things returned to normal. We listened to speakers after dinner and then went our separate ways. After evening snacks I joined Daniel and Stevie to smoke. I told them about Wayne taking my golf club.

"Tess probably beat the shit out of him in the

counselor's lounge," Stevie postulated.

"I doubt it was pleasant for him," Daniel said.

"When she gets home she'll kick the dog too. I love it," Stevie said.

Rollo and Big John joined us. Rollo's friend Robert was gone, as were the other of the barracudas, so Rollo was hanging with the old folks.

"Let's do something tonight," Rollo suggested.

"Wanna play cards?" Big John asked.

"No," he said, "something fun, something illegal."

Stevie leaned forward and whispered, "Let's go ghost hunting."

"Yeah," said Rollo.

"Up on the third floor, after lights out," she continued.

"Yeah," Rollo repeated.

"How do we get up there?" I asked her.

"Cowboy Bob is on duty until midnight. He leaves to lock doors about eleven twenty and takes his time about it. Darrell went home sick so there won't be anyone on the floor until Aaron comes on a few minutes past midnight. We could have a good thirty minutes to explore."

"Perfect," Rollo said, "let's do it."

"I'm in," I said. "Daniel? John?"

"I'm not going up," John said. "I don't want to make enemies of the dearly departed. I'll play lookout if you want, give you an all clear to come back down."

"Daniel," Stevie said, "Come along. Live a little."

"I don't believe in ghosts," he said.

"So look at the architecture," she told him. "Do it

because its fun. Do it because its against the rules."

He smiled. "Okay, I'm in."

We plotted the adventure and waited. About eleven thirty it seemed as if Cowboy Bob had gotten stuck at the hall desk and petrified there. Finally, his keys jingled. He came down to the smoking room and admonished us against turning on our room lights or the television. Stevie pointed out that we weren't in our rooms and that the smoking room didn't have a television. He told her to go to bed and she flipped him the bird behind his back as he left. A moment later he was gone.

"Let's go," Rollo said.

"Wait," warned John. He walked down the hall to where it turned, surveyed the dorm area and motioned for us to proceed. The stairway to the third floor was blocked only by a felt rope and a "Do Not Enter" sign. We ducked under it and took the stairs to the third floor.

The third floor was an exact image of the second floor dorm. We were on the short section that on the floors below led to the smoking room. It was dark, but the doors to the rooms were open allowing in a tiny amount of casual light from outside the Manor. We stood silent and motionless for a few moments letting our eyes adjust to the blackness.

Rollo moved first. He crossed the hall and peered through the nearest door. The room was furnished with a desk and chair as if someone had begun to set up an office and stopped halfway through. We moved past a couple of bathrooms and looked through the next open door. The room was empty.

"Here ghost, here ghost," Rollo whispered. Stevie hit him lightly on the side of his head. Daniel got tired of the sneaking and started walking boldly down the middle of the hall toward the point where it ended. Once there he could see down the long portion of the corridor where most the rooms were located. Stevie, Rollo, and I joined him.

We walked down the hall looking through each of the doors. A few of the rooms had a bed, but most were empty. The ceilings slanted over the rooms at the angle of the roof with gable windows extending outward.

"Here ghost, here ghost," Rollo said again.

"Shut up," Stevie said. "You'll scare him away."

As we proceeded we encountered an odor that was familiar, but I could not quite place it. "What's that smell?" I asked.

"The ghost," Stevie said. "I smelled the same thing in the infirmary when I saw him there."

"There's no ghost," Daniel said.

We were about half way down the hall when we heard a sound ahead of us.

"What was that?" Rollo asked.

"The ghost," Stevie said.

"There's someone down there," Daniel said. "We better go back."

"No," said Stevie. "It's the ghost. Let's go."

The four of us tiptoed toward the turn at the end of the long hall. When almost there we heard the sound again. This time there was a distinct groan and then a short gurgling sound. The odor in the air was stronger, an essence both sweet and acrid at the same time.

"Let's go back," Daniel said.

"No," Stevie ordered.

"C'mon Professor," Rollo said. "What can happen?" We turned the corner and tiptoed down the short leg of the hall opposite where we began. There was so little light in the corridor that I could barely see Rollo and Stevie. We heard something moving in one of the rooms on the right side. Everyone stopped to listen and the hall was silent again.

Stevie shoved Rollo and said "Go look." He moved forward and stuck his head in the first room on the right. He motioned with his hand to indicate that there was nothing unusual inside. We shuffled forward.

Rollo moved to the next door. He poked his head around the corner then pulled back as if he'd touched an electrical wire.

"There's someone there," he said. The three of us behind Rollo froze in place.

"Who?" asked Daniel.

"Somebody's on the floor by the bed."

"Look again," Stevie said.

"You look," he told her. Stevie moved forward. I went with her. The sickly odor in the hall was stronger. She leaned over and looked in. I poked my head over her shoulder to look with her.

Someone or something lay in a heap next to the bare mattress on the bed. I thought for a moment it was a duffel bag or pile of laundry. Then it moved. Stevie stood up and pulled back, hitting me in the chin with the back of her head.

"Sorry," she said, "it moved."

"I know," I told her, rubbing my wound.

The two of us leaned over and looked again. The odor from the room sent a wave of nausea up from my stomach. The lump inside had changed position but was motionless again. Stevie stepped inside. I held my position while Stevie moved closer trying to see in the dark. Daniel, Rollo, and I awaited word from her.

"It's Jack," Stevie said.

"It's Jack," I repeated. I stepped into the room behind Stevie. In the darkness I made out the figure of Jack on the floor. He had vomited on his clothes. Stevie reached down and picked something up. It was a quart bottle. She held it in a ray of light from the window. The label read "Imitation Vanilla Extract." Jack was drunk.

We ran downstairs without waiting for Big John's signal. We told John what we had found and decided it would be best for everyone to get to bed. I went to my room. The new linens were still stacked on Robert's bed.

16

I never saw Indian Jack again after the night of the ghost hunt. The following day Cowboy Bob took Jack's few belongings out of our room. In the aftermath of the fuss with Tess, Jack had gotten into the kitchen pantry and found the alcohol-laden vanilla extract. Using alcohol at the Manor meant instant expulsion, and Jack was gone by breakfast the next morning. The Manor was quiet that day. No one talked much. The smoking room was empty for most of the day.

My own stay at the Manor was coming to an end as well. Wayne had scheduled me for lifeline and my fifth step. In lifeline I would tell my life story—the good, the bad, and the pathetic—to the entire student body of the Manor. In fifth step I had to tell Sky Pilot everything I had written during step four.

The fifth step in AA required that I admit to God and to another person the exact nature of my wrongs. I figured that God had read over my shoulder as I wrote, thus I'd already admitted my wrongs to him. The other person was Sky Pilot. He heard all the fifth steps, because being of the clergy, he couldn't testify in court against his confessors. For many at the Manor, including me, this was important.

During that quiet day after Indian Jack's departure I thought about lifeline and my upcoming fifth step. One by one, the things I'd written in my fourth step came back to me. I divided the events of my life by their wince factors. If remembering some distasteful event on my trip to the Manor made me wince just once I could include it in lifeline. The single wincers could stay. The double and triple wincers, however, would remain secret until I got to Sky Pilot.

I had become willing to do both my lifeline and the fifth step, but my willingness did not alleviate my fear of finally telling the truth about myself. For many years truth had been a shrouded monster in the distance. I was terrified of it. Through group and my fourth step I had seen the monster up close, and it was not so terrible and awesome as it seemed. It was ugly, but nothing to be terrified of. Nevertheless, there was only a certain amount of the ugliness that I was willing to show to others.

After dinner I sat for a while alone in the non-smoking lounge. I picked up a Bible from among the Readers Digest condensed books on the bookcase. The Bible was an inexpensive hardback with color plates in the middle. I thought of my three Bibles at home. One I received in the third grade as a reward for successfully completing Sunday school. I kept it as a memento of my childhood. The second was a King James version that sat on a shelf in my apartment next to a volume of Bible commentary that was thicker than the Bible itself. This Bible I had studied. The third was a modern English version I had picked up at a garage sale. It was a quick reference for looking things up in a hurry. The first was a souvenir, the second an academic text, and the third a reference book. The one in the Manor lounge was none of these things.

I opened the Bible to Matthew and started reading. I didn't read critically or even carefully. I let the words flow over me. I cared less for the sense of them than for the sound of them in my head. The verses calmed me, and took my mind off the upcoming lifeline. I finished Matthew and went to bed. Remembering how it felt to read the scriptures I fell asleep.

Lifeline happened at four-thirty the following afternoon. I'd made an outline on one of my legal pads with good things listed on the left, the negative on the right. I graduated from undergraduate school at approximately the same time I began to drink every day. Graduation went on the left. The drinking went on the right. I established my own law practice and promptly missed my first court date because of a hangover. My practice was on the left, the missed appearance on the right. As my alcohol and drug use increased the right side of the pages began to dominate the left. The outline ended with my admission to the Manor. The jury was still out on which side of the page that belonged.

I wasn't overly nervous about lifeline until I actually got into the meditation room and saw the others waiting. People were laughing and talking. Normally I'd have been joking with them, but on that day I felt alone.

"Counselor," Big John asked, "are you ready?"

"As I'll ever be," I told him.

"Did you put in some good sex stuff?" Stevie asked. "That time with the two midgets and the sheep."

"Yeah Stevie," I said, "I put that in just for you."

"Oh, goody," she said.

Wayne came in and called us to order. We started

with the serenity prayer. I listened as the group said it in unison for the thousandth time, "God, grant me the serenity to accept the things I cannot change, the courage to change the things I can, and the wisdom to know the difference."

Wayne quieted the group after the prayer and I began. Things started out fine. I talked through my college days and my days in San Francisco. I talked relatively easily about the heavy drinking during law school and being awarded my doctorate while drunk. Telling how I had lost my career was more difficult. I'd had a profession and I'd drowned it in alcohol. It was still hard for me to look at that, much less tell a room full of people about it. My failed career in law, however, was not the worst. Most of the drunks and addicts at the Manor had somehow managed to keep their addictions as well as a job. They were impaired but employed, and their employers, through insurance, were paying the Manor bill with a hope of getting them back. They had people waiting. I did not. For two years I'd holed up in my apartment to drink. My insurance came from Isol's work. I hadn't left a job to come to the Manor, and I didn't have one to return to.

The years of isolated drinking were the most difficult to speak of. My voice cracked when I spoke about how I'd abandoned my parents and my friends, and my profession. I'd failed to support my wife or even carry out simple household duties around the apartment. Bills went unpaid and phone calls went unanswered while I drank. Tears came to my eyes. I told them I was afraid that during those two years I'd forgotten how to live. No one knew me except Isol, the people at the Manor, and a few barflies. There was no world to which I could return.

By the end of lifeline I was crying openly and the group was silent. "Let's call it a day," Wayne said. People rose and came over to pat me on the shoulder. Their sympathy was genuine. No one cared what I'd done, but telling my story still hurt. After dinner that evening I joined Daniel in the smoking room.

"I graduate tomorrow," he said.

"I know," I told him. "I'm the day after. Have you signed my Big Book?" Signing Big Books was part of the ritual of leaving.

"Yesterday," he said.

"Are you going back to teaching?" I asked.

"I'll be back there Monday."

"It must be nice," I said.

"What are you going to do?"

"I don't know."

"Can you go back to law?"

"Well, I'm not disbarred, if that's what you mean. The Bar would probably let me back in but I doubt anyone would give me a job."

"Can you start your own practice?"

"In theory," I said, "but that takes cash and desire. I don't have any of either."

"You didn't like being a lawyer, did you?"

"Nobody likes being a lawyer. We do it for the money."

"It looks like fun on TV," he said. Stevie and John came in and lit cigarettes.

"So what's up?" Stevie asked.

"We're plotting the future," Daniel said. "What about you, Stevie? Are you going back to real estate when you get out?"

"Nope," she said. "I'm gonna be a housewife."

"That's a frightful thought," Big John said.

"Kiss off. I have a house. I am a wife. Why the hell can't I be a housewife?"

"Okay, you're a housewife," John said.

"I'll kick your ass," she said to him. "What are you going to do?"

"Two more years on the docks and I retire. Then I run for mayor."

"I'll vote for you," Daniel said.

"How about you professor?" Stevie said to Daniel. "Back to the classroom?"

"Yeah," Daniel said, "and by the way, I don't know why I'm the professor around here. I'm not the one with all the degrees."

"A lot of good they did me," I said.

"Why don't you teach?" Stevie asked me.

"I can't," I told her. "I don't have the temperament. I get a certain pleasure out of learning from others, but I don't like people to learn from me. I don't even correct people who mispronounce my name. It's not so much that I want people to stay ignorant; I just don't want them to get their knowledge from me. I will teach for short periods of time if someone really wants to learn and asks me for help, but even then I sometimes feel that by giving it away I might lose it."

"That's selfish," Stevie said.

"Yeah," Daniel added, "and you'd never make it as a teacher if you wait around for students who want to learn."

"So there's another thing I can't do?" I said.

"The nice thing about self pity," Stevie told me, "is that it's always sincere."

"Kiss off," I said.

"That's better. You've still got fifth step. Can't lose that stiff upper lip now."

"I do it tomorrow," I told her.

"Well say 'Hi' to Sky Pilot for me."

"How did yours go?" I asked Daniel.

"Long," he said. "I wrote for a long time on my fourth so there was a lot to deal with. My fourth was the deepest look at myself I've ever taken. I think I understand now why I did some of the things I did. I know why I needed cocaine."

"I know why, too," John said, "because you liked getting loaded."

"I mean," Daniel said, "I know why I wanted to be loaded. I can't really explain it, but I understand it."

"What John may be asking, in his own strange way," I said, "is does your knowing enable you to stop."

"I think so," he said.

"Well, did telling Sky Pilot about it help?" Stevie asked.

"It helped me formulate it. He seemed to agree with a lot of my conclusions. He thinks I've got it."

"Give it to me then," I said. "How did you handle the God stuff?"

"The pastor and I differ in approaches. His views

are traditional. I see God in all things, including myself. We don't believe in the same kind of God."

"Well I don't believe in God at all," I said. "What do I do?"

"Just be honest with him. He's all right."

"Do you think you can live sober?"

"I believe I can."

"He's got it," Stevie said. "Remember. He said so."

"How about you John?" I asked.

"The Morning Glory AA meetings start at seven o'clock every morning," he said. "I will be there every day."

"But will you be there sober?" Stevie asked.

"Alkies who go to the meetings and do the Big Book don't drink," he said. "Those who don't, do."

"So you've got it too?" she asked.

"I've got it today. That's what counts."

I asked Daniel, "Are you going to go to AA?"

"I'm going tomorrow night after I get out of here. I'll probably choose a Narcotics Anonymous group as my home group, but I want to explore all the AA groups. I'll see John at the Morning Glory and, hopefully, I will see all of you at one group or another."

"How about you Stevie?" I said.

"I'm gonna go," she told me.

"She'll probably start her own chapter," John said.

"Do that," I suggested to her.

"So will I," Daniel said. "We could all go together."

That night I had a drinking dream.

17

The morning after the using dream I was angry at having been put through lifeline. I blamed the nightmare on lifeline, and I blamed lifeline on the Manor. I didn't want to do step five.

The nasty little secrets that I'd included in my fourth step took turns bothering me. I started doubting the wisdom of telling my personal disgraces to someone else. Those doubts started me asking what the hell I was doing at the Manor anyway. If alcoholism was a disease, as they'd gone to great lengths to prove, then why hadn't I seen a doctor since that first physical? If they weren't pushing religion, why had I developed the God problem, and why was I about to make some huge confession to a minister I hardly knew?

"What if this is all just voodoo?" I asked Daniel as we smoked after breakfast.

"If what is voodoo?" he said.

"The stuff here," I said, "the program, the Big Book, the higher power, all of it?"

"What's wrong with voodoo?" he asked.

"It's weird," I said. "It's not real."

"Maybe," Daniel said, "but don't be too quick to judge voodoo. Voodoo, or magic if you prefer, was curing people long before the first scientist donned his pocket protector."

"You mean that I'm being treated by witch doctors."

"Maybe. Witch doctors and medical doctors come from the same root. Both have the same motives—to understand and control the forces of nature. For the magician, disease is animate and the spirit of the disease can be manipulated or even driven away. The medical doctor is attuned to the physics of disease, and by tinkering with the structure of the body tries to make his patient well again.

"Sadly, witch doctors have been done in by definitions. We define magic as either illusion, like the rabbit in the hat, or failed science, like good luck charms and leeches. If it works it's science. If it doesn't it's magic. By definition, the magician is a failure."

"If I do a rain dance and it rains, is it then science?"

"Not if the dance affects the spirit of rain. You'd still be a magician, albeit a successful one. A shaman will wash evil spirits from his skin before laying hands on a patient. A medical doctor will wash his hands to remove bacteria. The acts are similar, but motives make a difference. The successful magician is revered and elevated to a position equal to the king. The successful doctor gets a Mercedes."

"Why doesn't the doctor get to be equal the king?"

"Doctors are not attuned to the spirit. People don't like them. We reward them with money and respect, but not power."

"So where are the magicians now days? I may need one."

"They have a hard time of it. Scientists debunk them. Priests call them evil. Some read palms or tarot cards. Most go into social work or politics."

"Is there enough science here at the Manor to cure me?"

"Yes and no. Here, they practice a science of miracles. Statistically, treatment fails. Only one in ten of us will stay sober for a year. But for the one who stays sober it's both a miracle and as scientific as aspirin. I plan on being one of the sober ones. It is scientific enough for me."

"Sounds like Zen koans to me. I'd rather take a pill and be well."

Daniel was called away to see his counselor for his exit interview. His comments about the poor success rate at the Manor irritated me. We all knew that only one or two of us would be able to stay sober for a year. Like everyone else, I desperately wanted to know what it was that allowed one person stay sober when another could not. How did a person become the one?

Daniel's logic, or lack of it, was unsatisfying. It seemed to me that medicine took little interest in addicts. I didn't blame science. I had no feeling that doctors had some intrinsic obligation to waste time in this distasteful and unprofitable area. However, it meant that treatment fell into the hands of a few do-gooders and the addicts themselves. These were not people who inspired a lot of confidence. Those who were recovering nursed the users into sobriety. Places like the Manor boasted the highest recovery rate in the field, largely I suspected, because they were the only ones in it. Sobriety was a gift. It might be given to me, but I could not earn it. Maybe I already had it. If I didn't, at least my chances of getting it were better in the program than outside of it.

Before lunch we gathered for Daniel's graduation.

His regular counselor was ill, and Tess had selected herself to do the honors. Daniel's parents were the only outsiders present. They sat on one of the ornate couches against the wall looking uncomfortable amidst the alkies and addicts. Daniel accosted me in the hall, led me to his parents, and introduced me as his friend.

"I'm pleased to meet you both," I said. We shook hands.

"I've heard a lot about you," his mother said. "I know you've helped Daniel."

I wondered what Daniel had told them. I was embarrassed in front of them and they were embarrassed in front of me. Despite the disease model we all promised to honor, Daniel's parents were embarrassed because they were in a room full of failures.

Tess called the proceedings to order, and on cue, Daniel joined her in front of the crowd. She recounted briefly the changes Daniel had undergone since coming to the Manor. His hands had ceased shaking. His depression was gone. He had become useful and productive by helping new patients. At the end of the testimonial Tess gave him a Malady Manor coin and a written program to keep him occupied and sober on the outside. While the patients applauded his passing, Tess stiffly gave him a hug. I prepared myself for something profound, but Daniel disappointed me. He turned and said, "I want to thank all of you, and wish everyone sobriety." That was it.

Stevie and I were at the front of the line to give Daniel his good-by squeeze. "Hi," he said when I approached. For a moment we were sad together. The sabbatical was over. He was going outside where the liquor flowed and the cocaine passes hands in tavern bathrooms. I was going there too. I hugged him. Although we'd sworn we would reunite on the outside, I suspected that I'd never see him again.

I sat next to Stevie at lunch. Daniel was gone. "Do you think he'll make it?" I asked her.

"I think we're all going to make it," she said. "Our group is going to be the exception."

"No, seriously," I said.

"I think he will," she said, "but it would be easier for him without those parents. They blame him."

"They're straight," I said. "They can't help it."

"Maybe not, but it will still be tough to stay sober with them around."

"I don't think he'll make it," I said.

"Why not?"

"I don't know?" I told her, "I just don't think he's the one."

I was changing my shoes for exercise when Cowboy Bob showed up in my room. "The minister is ready for you," he said.

"I'll be right there," I answered. I took the stack of legal pads from the bottom drawer of my desk and went downstairs. Sky Pilot's door was open.

"Come in," he said. He was sitting in the same place he had been during our first abortive conversation about God.

"How are you?" I asked. I took the seat across from him.

"Fine, and yourself."

"Okay."

"Is your fourth step done?"

"Yes."

"Are you satisfied with it?"

"It's as complete as I can make it." I held up the stack of yellow pads.

"Do you want to read it or just tell it?"

"I want to read."

He proceeded to assure me that anything I said during the fifth step could never be repeated anywhere and that even the law could not compel him to testify. I knew the law and trusted his promise of secrecy.

"Well let's go," I said. I picked up the first pad and began to read. Never before in an oral presentation had I ever used my written text as any more than a guide to what I might say, but this time I read word for word. Sky Pilot remained silent.

I told him everything I'd ever felt guilty about. I told him about errors and omissions in childhood—small things that had left big memories. I told him about the people I'd hurt and the people who had hurt me. I told him about being a lawyer and the lies and injustices I had abetted in the name of the profession. I told him about drinking.

The emotions I felt while writing rushed back at me, but my voice didn't crack, and I shed no tears. As I finished each yellow pad I put it at my feet. Three hours after starting, I put the last one down.

Sky Pilot looked me in the eyes. "Do you have anything else you want to say, anything at all?" he asked.

"That's all," I said.

"Will you pray with me?" I agreed. We bowed our heads. He proceeded to recite the Lord's Prayer. When the prayer ended we both were silent. After a couple of minutes of listening to the clock tick he asked. "What do you plan to do when you leave here?"

"I don't know," I said.

"Will you practice law?"

"Maybe."

"Is there something else you can turn to?" he asked. "It seems that the legal profession requires a person to do many unpleasant things." He was referring to that part of my fifth step where I had confessed the sins of lawyering. By maneuver and machination I had enabled people to avoid just debts and collected money from people who shouldn't have had to pay. I'd deprived parents of their children and children of their parents. I'd caused crimes to go unpunished. All of it was legal but I never argued that it was justice. I did it for the money, but money does not relieve guilt. Guilt always got its due.

"It is not a pleasant profession," I said.

"Could you teach?" he asked. People were always trying to make me a teacher. I wondered why people always suggested teaching as an option for those who had failed at everything else.

"Maybe," I said, not wanting to debate with him. He took the cue.

"Tradition here is that we burn your fourth step. It's not required. Some people prefer to keep it. If you . . . ."

"I'll burn it," I interrupted.

"Fine," he said. "Let's go." I gathered my stack of yellow paper. We left the Manor through the front door and went to a rusted burn barrel at the edge of the Manor grounds. When we reached the barrel Sky Pilot took the pads from me and put them atop a pile of soggy ashes inside. He produced a pack of matches, and bending over to reach inside lit one corner of the top pad. The burning sheets turned black and curled, exposing new sheets as the top one turned to ash.

"God," said Sky Pilot, "allow the pain, anger and resentments contained in these pages to be carried away with the smoke from this fire." We watched it burn. After a few minutes Sky Pilot said, "I'm going back in. You may stay here." He put his arm around my shoulder for a second and then left for his office.

I stood alone over the barrel and watched the paper being consumed. I could hear the sounds of the city in the distance. The white smoke from the fire floated up over the Manor and disappeared.

When the last flame died down I walked to the picnic table by the volleyball court. I sat on the table and stared at the Manor. Trees were in bloom. The late afternoon sun was warm on my skin. I felt empty. I'd been scoured inside. For the moment I had no past or future. Everything I ever was or would be was wrapped up in the moment, in the sensations of the Manor grounds and the late spring afternoon. I felt as if in the effort to rid myself of the craving for drugs, I'd lost everything that had been me.

The sun disappeared behind the trees, and as the

air cooled I started to shiver. I smoked one last cigarette and went back to the Manor. When I reached my
room there was a new suitcase on the bed next to mine.
I would have a new roommate for the night. I went to
the smoking room hoping to avoid meeting him until
after dinner.

"How'd it go?" Stevie asked at dinner.

"No problem," I said.

"Do you feel any different?"

"No," I lied.

"Did he ask you any questions?"

"No."

"Do you want to talk about it?"

"No."

"If you change your mind . . . ."

I met my new roommate after dinner. His name
was Albert. He was sixty-two years old and hard of
hearing. Unable to hear his own words, he yelled when
he spoke. I didn't like him because he meant my time at
the Manor was over.

I called Isol. "I get off work at eleven," she said, "so
I'll be there in plenty of time."

"Good," I said. "I look forward to seeing you."

"Did anything happen today?"

"Not much," I told her. "Daniel graduated."

"Oh, good for him. I hope we can see him some
more when you are out."

"We probably will." I turned the conversation to
things at home. "I love you," I said when my phone
time was about up, "I truly do."

"I love you too," she said. "I want you home again."

18

On the morning of my graduation I stood in the smoking room staring through the trees at the bit of city visible from the Manor. I could see glimpses of the early morning traffic. Despite the cold, I opened the window. If I listened carefully I could hear the sounds of the morning commute. I was going home, not just to Isol and the apartment, but home to the city.

During my morning shower it struck me how dingy and confining the Manor had become. All the people who had helped me through the first days were gone. Most of the rooms contained strangers who were still confused and detoxing. I sympathized with each of them, but not one of them would become my friend.

"Are you going to stay here forever?" I asked Big John at breakfast. "You were here when I got here. Now I'm leaving and you're still at it."

"I'm a thirty-day kind of guy. More if I need it," he said. "Union benefits. I have four days left and I plan to enjoy every one of them."

"You enjoy everything, John. I'm ready to go."

"Are you going to be the one who makes it?" he asked. I shrugged. I didn't know.

After breakfast I had an exit interview with Wayne. I'd liked Wayne from the first day, but during my stay I'd also grown to respect him. In his way he was a wise young man. He recognized the extent of his own abilities and was comfortable living within those limits. I had never been able to do that. He didn't expect his patients to change, but if they did he was genuinely pleased for them. When I first met him I envied his sobriety. As he sat thumbing through papers preparing for my graduation I envied his wisdom.

"Do you have any last drawings?" he asked. I turned over my final bunch. He paged through them, savoring each one. "I love these things," he said. "I can follow you through the steps, just by the drawings. You ought to do this kind of thing for a living."

"Sure," I said, "if my movie career doesn't work out, I'll get a job drawing cartoons of drunks. I hear there's a big market for that."

"You have a talent for it," he said. He always ignored sarcasm.

If I keep drawing the pictures will I stay sober?"

"Maybe. What do you plan to do when you get out?" I was seriously tired of that question.

"I'm going to look for a job," I told him.

"Good," he said. He began writing on the form in front of him. "I'm making you an aftercare program. Try to follow it as closely as possible. You are to spend your mornings looking for work."

"Okay."

"What kind of exercise do you like?" He had his finger on the next line of the form.

"Golf," I said.

"Can you play twice a week?"

"I'd love it." I didn't mention that I didn't have enough money to play twice a month.

"What other exercise do you like?"

"Smoking," I said.

"Seriously."

"Okay, maybe basketball." I hadn't played basketball in years.

"Where?"

"There's a park near my place."

"Twice a week for at least thirty minutes."

"Okay," I said.

"We have aftercare meetings here on Wednesday evenings and Saturday mornings. Which group would you like?"

"Wednesday. What are those about?"

"Graduates meet for an hour or so. You talk about how it's going in sobriety. You'll be lonely out there if you don't get hooked up with sober people."

"What about my regular friends?"

"You can see them," he said, "but try to stay away from taverns and the places you used to drink. You don't have to give up your friends, but if you don't use, they will eventually give up on you."

"Well they won't if I'm not an asshole about the fact that I can't drink."

I had a plan. When Smugger had learned I was going in for the treatment he warned me not to come out self-righteous. The other Lemmings shared his concern. I figured that if I kept my sobriety to myself I'd be fine, and I could still be one of the Lemmings. I'd be the sober one. Crusaders who had given up one vice or another and then become raving assholes about it had annoyed me often enough. I was determined not to become one of them.

"Some friends may stick with you," Wayne said. He didn't look like he believed it. "But you'll need an AA group."

"Okay."

"There's a group for lawyers."

"I haven't been a lawyer for three years," I said, "and I wasn't that great a lawyer when I was doing it."

"Well, it's a thought." The best thing for you is to go to a meeting every day for the first ninety days. Go when you want to go and go when you don't want to go. The meetings will keep you sober while you work the rest of your steps." He handed me a pamphlet listing times and locations of AA meetings throughout the city.

"Go to different ones at first. Find a group where you are comfortable and stick with it. You need a home group as a base."

"Do I sign up or something?"

"The only requirement for membership is a desire to stop drinking. They'll tell you that. Your home group is wherever you decide to go."

"Do you still go?" I asked.

"I'll go a lot," he said. "The meetings show me how to live sober. I like them. After a while, going to meetings is no longer a chore; it's a reprieve."

"How poetic," I said.

"Each group has a temperament. You need to find one you are comfortable with. Some are pure Big Book. Some are religious. Others incorporate ideas from a variety of sources. There's one group in town made up primarily of atheists who need the program but can't stomach God. If you really want to stay sober, there's a group close to where you live that will do it if any group can. It doesn't have any official name, but people in the program call it Murdock's. It's AA with an attitude. Pure Big Book, no bullshit. They preach the Big Book and people who go there stay sober. The place is short on sympathy but respected for its successes. Murdock's takes the tough cases. It might not be your kind of place for a home group, but you ought to go a couple of times to see them in action."

"Sure," I said. I filed the name Murdock's in the keeper portion of my remaining memory. "Wayne," I said. "What does my file say? How did I do here?"

"In what sense?"

"Did I pass? Did I get an 'A' in recovery? Will I stay sober?"

"You get an 'A,'" he said, "but you've always gotten 'A's."

"Not always."

"I told you when you came here that lawyers are tough nuts to crack. To tell the truth, no one here believes you. We discuss each of the patients in staff meetings. When your file comes up, you've always said and done the right things, but no one believes it. If you've been truthful here, you're the Cassandra of recovery. From a clinical perspective your performance has been flawless. Your performance in lifeline brought tears to the eyes of every person in that room. I was moved, but later I wondered whether any of it was true."

It was the first time in years that I told the truth, and no one believed me. There was an odd justice to it. "Sincerity is the key, baby," I said to Wayne. "Once you can fake that, you've got it made."

"That's what I mean. You're an artist one moment and a cynic the next. Everyone here sees someone different when they look at you. Patty, for example, thinks you're a Catholic."

"Catholicism has some strong points."

"Well, your explanation of the strong points of Catholicism may have convinced her to return to the church. I haven't had the heart to tell her that you don't believe a word of it."

"I believed it when I talked to her. The belief didn't last."

"And that whole thing with the golf club. What was that?"

"Recreation."

"Well, it made for an interesting staff meeting afterward."

"Pleased to be entertaining," I said.

"It really doesn't matter if anyone here knows who you are. You can hide from us if you want. What counts is that you have some idea who you are, or at least who you want to be."

"Is that important?"

"The books say so. You can't accept yourself until you understand who you are."

"I have no idea who I am. I thought I knew when I came here. Now I'm sure I don't know."

"Don't think about it. Who do you feel you are?"

"I don't feel, remember."

"You told me you'd started feeling."

"I did, I guess. I feel empty like a tuba. If you blow on me I can make sound, but it's still only empty brass tubing. I feel sensations—hot and cold—but the feelings don't mean anything to me. I felt sad for Daniel when he left, but I don't know why. Then the feeling was gone and I was empty again. I don't know what to do from one minute to the next. Everything I knew about myself is gone; all the things I believed were wrong. I don't believe my beliefs any more and they were all I had. Sky Pilot did it. He stole my soul."

"How do you feel about leaving?"

"I want to go. It's a sunny day. I want to walk home and look at the city."

"Do you want a drink?"

"No."

"You will later. Say no to it and go to a meeting. Do the rest of the twelve steps. The AA group will help you stay away from the booze. The steps will take away the craving."

"When?" I asked.

"When you've done them all. Not perfectly, mind you, but to the best of your ability."

"You sound like Big John. I'll do what I can though. I do want to stay sober."

"Just wanting it isn't enough. You have to finish the program."

"I will," I said. "I truly appreciate your trying to help me. You can keep the drawings."

"Thanks," Wayne said, "You can pick up your pitching wedge after graduation. It's behind the reception desk."

For graduation I put on a dress shirt, wool slacks, and a pair of Florsheims. It was the first time since coming to the Manor that I'd donned anything other than jeans and a sweatshirt. The dress clothes felt good. I sat at the desk and sorted my unread novels and drawing materials into piles appropriate for packing. The fact of my departure became real. Time had stood still for three weeks. The clock was about to start ticking again.

"His hands were shaking so badly he couldn't hold a spoon. His blood pressure was so high we were considering hospitalization." Wayne was giving his speech about me—the standard where-he-came-from-and-how-far-he's-come stuff that everyone got at graduation. I stood next to him. The patients were there. Isol sat in the front row holding a dozen roses. She was a beautiful woman, even after all we had been through. She looked comfortable and proud in her tailored work clothes. Unlike Daniel's parents, she was at ease with the patients. She held the roses across her breast. "He changed more in his time here than anyone I've known. His drawings have delighted the patients, the staff . . . ."

Big John and Stevie were sitting together behind Isol. They were filled with potential giggles, expecting me to drop my pants or something equally outrageous. I planned to disappoint them. I didn't have a lot of respect for graduations, but I had never disrupted one either.

"Your turn," Wayne said. I had the floor.

"I've learned something here," I said. "I've learned it from those of you here and the ones who were here when I arrived. I've learned that I'm not alone with my addiction. There are lots of us. To me that makes a difference. I'm afraid of being alone, and, if I'm not alone, none of you are either. I don't have to fight this thing one-on-one. I'm allowed help, and from now on I'm enlisting all the help I can get. Thanks for your help."

They applauded.

After my speech Wayne gave me my Manor coin and an envelope with the aftercare program he'd been working on that morning. We shook hands and the line formed behind him for hugs. Isol was first in line. Stevie stood behind her holding the flowers. Tears were running down Isol's face. She leaped on me like an exuberant three year old. "Congratulations," she said. "Welcome home."

"Thanks," I said. I held her tight against me. "I'll be there soon." Stevie was next.

"I'll miss you, you son-of-a-bitch," she said. "Stay straight for me. Show 'em your stuff."

"I will," I told her.

Big John and the rest then took turns giving me hugs and wishing me the best. When it was over Isol was still there holding the roses.

"You look great," she said.

"Thanks," I told her. I held out my hand, palm down. "Look, solid as a rock."

"You've gained weight too. Your eye's sparkle."

"I feel good."

"These are for you." She handed me the roses. I stood there awkwardly holding the flowers. We stood for a moment staring at each other.

"What do I do with these now?" I asked.

"Here," Stevie broke in. "I'll put them in your room. You two go to lunch."

Isol and I left the Manor through the front door as the others were preparing for lunch. I felt like a schoolboy sneaking away from class. The Manor rules had settled on me. It didn't feel right to be leaving.

"What do you want to eat?" Isol asked.

"Mexican," I said, "the hotter the better." We got into the pickup and Isol drove to a Mexican diner a few blocks from the Manor. As we sat at the counter waiting for food I felt once again the emptiness that had followed me since the fifth step. I had no idea what to say to Isol. I wanted her to know what had happened to me, but I really didn't understand it myself. We made small talk. I had the feeling that Isol was testing me—trying to find out if the person she knew was still there. She was pleased to be with me, but uneasy. I wanted to reassure her, but I didn't know how. I didn't know if I could.

"I cleaned all the alcohol out of the house," she told me. "There's no pot, nothing."

"That's good," I said.

When we finished eating, Isol dropped me back at the Manor and returned to work. I picked up my golf club from the receptionist and went to my room to pack. The other patients were corralled in the dining room watching a film. My pens and paper were still arranged on my desk. I took the clothes I'd worn for the last three weeks and shoved them in my duffel bag. On top of the clothes I put the novels and the aftercare envelope. I put the duffel bag and the golf club, all my worldly possessions, on the bed next to the roses. I planned to walk home and come back for them later. The possessions could wait. For a few hours I didn't want anything weighing me down.

Alcoholics use the term "pink cloud" to describe that period of elation that accompanies new sobriety. The moment I stepped out the Manor door the pink cloud hit me like a kick in the sternum. The afternoon sun had heated the pavement and I felt the warmth of the sidewalk through my shoes. The sunlight tasted like candy.

I walked down one of the side streets in the industrial area past auto parts warehouses and wholesale food outlets. The windowless buildings concealed the commerce within, but activity reverberated in the air. Men with fork lifts and pallet jacks unloaded trucks onto docks that had old tires hanging on the edges to cushion the cement from the impact of sixteen wheelers. Everything felt new: the warmth of the sun, the odor of trucks, the sounds of a train in the distance. My senses became electric. Feelings stirred, burst, and disappeared. I'd been emptied out at the Manor. As I walked, the void inside began to fill. For the first time in years I experienced wonder.

Home was two miles away. The street that led home housed the kind of businesses that do just fine with dirty windows and unswept doorways. I stared through each window, marveling at the dry cleaners, upholsterers, and printers who populated the industrial area. Foot traffic was nonexistent. These were the kind of places one drives to out of necessity and gets out of as quickly as business can be done.

After half a mile or so, the nature of the businesses changed. Small Asian groceries, lunch counters catering to men who wore steel toed boots, and taverns peaked out from between the warehouses.

The first tavern was the Lone Wolf. I stopped and looked. I could remember the place from my previous life. I knew what it was like inside. I knew how the tables were arranged, where the pool tables stood, and where the beer was poured. I knew it would be cool and dark inside.

I was alone. No one would have to know if I stopped in for a drink. A barkeep's vow of silence is at least as sacred as the one Sky Pilot had given. If no one knew, what would it matter? A couple of brews and then I would start on sobriety.

I walked into a small diner run by an Asian couple. The menu, written in marker on a board behind the ice cream machine, touted teriyaki and chiliburgers. The place was empty except for the man-and-wife proprietors. I ordered fries and a Seven-up from the diminutive Chinese waitress who yelled the order to her coworker-husband. The greasy fries were heaven to me after the three weeks of low fat, low salt fare at the Manor. The Seven-up hurt my mouth. I sipped it to let my membranes readjust to carbonation. When I was done eating and had paid up my tiny waitress said, "You come back now." It was a Texas farewell delivered in a staccato Asian accent—more an order than an invitation.

I left the diner and wandered off into a residential area. Lawns sprouted dandelions and overgrew the sidewalks. Stalwart residents mowed and weeded in their yards. The less resolute hid inside leaving the battle to landlords or Mexicans with pickups. I gulped in the sights, seeing everything for the first time.

As I came closer to home the businesses were replaced by single family dwellings and then small apartment complexes with names like Greenbriar Court and Laurelhurst Manor. The neighborhood was dotted with parks where the basketball courts were always full and the ethnic cultures of the city mixed nervously. On the courts black men grunted out fantasies of the NBA. On the green expanses of grass Vietnamese families tended their round-faced youngsters and ate food from baskets. Walking down a street across from one of the parks I came upon an old man struggling with a lawn mower. He had just mowed the median strip in front of his apartment. He was small, thin, and unable to heft the rusty push mower back up the few steps to the apartment.

"Do you need some help?" I asked. Suspicion swept across his face.

"Can you pull this up the stairs?" he asked.

"Sure," I said. He stepped aside, and in a moment I had the mower to the top of the stairs.

"Do you live around here?" the old man asked. "I haven't seen you before."

"A few blocks south of here," I told him. "I don't get out much."

"I've lived here twenty-two years," he said. "People

don't help out like they used to. Thank you."

"You're welcome," I said. I was proud of my good deed. It had been a long time since I'd done something for someone else. He disappeared into the apartment.

Within an two hours of leaving the Manor I was home. I shivered when I looked at the outside of the apartment where I'd done my drinking. Isol had cleaned out the booze and the hash pipes, but the walls held memories. Inside it looked the same as before. I sat on the couch. The elation and sense of wonder that I felt outside drained away. My feeling of communion with the world dissolved and I was empty again.

I got a soda from the refrigerator and returned to the couch. Carbonation still hurt my mouth. I put the can on the coffee table in front of me where I had put thousands of Budweisers in the years before.

When Isol returned we drove up to the Manor to retrieve my duffel bag. At the Manor I thought I had so much to say to her, so much explaining, so many apologies, but when I was home the things I had to say were gone. I, who was so educated and opinionated, had nothing to say. I was lost in my own life. I sensed that I loved her, but not knowing who or where I was, I wasn't sure. Fortunately, she was patient. We were together again, and I was home. That, for a while, would be enough.

19

The days that followed my stay at the Manor were days of grieving. Drugs and alcohol had been my closest and dearest loves. I had been with them longer than I'd lived with my parents. I'd stayed with them through marriage, divorce, and remarriage. They'd outlasted all my jobs. Nothing in my life had been with me as long as liquor. When it left, I grieved.

For the first few days I followed directions and stayed away from everything associated with my old life. I called the Lemmings, but I didn't go see them. My shadow did not darken the tavern doors. I followed the dictates of the Big Book, avoiding the slippery places that might entice me back to the bottle. But in the end I could not grieve that way. I needed closure. I had to visit the grave of my loved one.

I walked into Taps just before noon on my fifth day out. The barkeeps were cleaning tables and cooking for the small lunch crowd. I knew everyone who worked there. I knew their spouses and the kind of lives they lived. Seeing me come in, they stopped what they were doing and gathered at the bar to ask what it had been like and how I was doing. My Seven-Up was on the house. They offered me support and best wishes. I felt the warmth of a homecoming, but in truth it was a farewell. We all knew that if I really stopped drinking I'd stop coming to Taps. If I started again, I'd have to drink somewhere else. We were going separate ways.

In the months that followed I visited Taps many times. Sometimes I would get a burger or just read the paper. Often, after picking up Isol from work, we would stop in and have a soda while the Lemmings quaffed a few brews. The visits, however, were short and unsatisfying. What had once been easy and natural had become awkward and stilted. Without alcohol to lubricate the conversation I had little to say. I became impatient and irritable. We tapered off the visits and life at Taps went on without us.

I began going to AA the day after I was released from the Manor. I kept the small directory of AA groups that Wayne had given me and had committed to attending ninety meetings in my first ninety days. Finding an AA group was not so different from finding the right tavern; I walked into groups and waited for one to choose me. At first I felt awkward going to AA meetings, as if I was invading someone else's living room. At the meeting down the street from the public detox center, I felt awkward because I'd never lived on the streets. Up at the Seventh Day Adventist Hospital I felt awkward because I hadn't graduated from the hospital's treatment center. At the Native American meeting I felt awkward because I was white. At the well-heeled lawyers meeting I felt awkward because I was broke. And then I went to Murdock's.

Murdock's was housed in a small storefront appended to a Victorian home on the edge of the warehouse district. By the time I got there the Victorian house had been made into apartments and the street-level retail space, identified by nothing more than a street number, had been made into Murdock's.

I went to Murdock's for the five thirty after-work

meeting. The single room inside was a ramshackle meeting hall furnished with the donations of people who didn't have much to give. Theatre seats leaned against one wall still attached to each other so that people sitting there shared arm rests. On the opposite wall the attendees lounged on overstuffed sofas. The rest of the room held unmatched kitchen chairs arranged around small writing tables. A teacher's desk with a gavel and AA books sat at the head of this makeshift semicircle. The meetings were run from that desk.

My first appearance at Murdock's went unnoticed by the members. People there knew each other but paid little attention to strangers. They left me alone. The meeting was different from others I had tried. At most meetings, including the mock meetings at the Manor, people would introduce themselves as alcoholics before speaking, and the whole room would then respond with "Hi, Bob" or "Hi, Mary" as a forced but genial welcome to the party. At Murdock's there was none of that. They got right down to business, letting you say "hi" to people on your own time.

The meeting proceeded according to the iron hand of Murdock's tradition. The Twelve Traditions of AA were read aloud. The Twelve Steps were read aloud. Newcomers were welcomed and it was solemnly announced that "The program of Alcoholics Anonymous is founded in the pages of the Big Book. Only AA speaks for AA. The opinions expressed in this room are those of the person expressing them. If what you hear cannot be reconciled with the Big Book, it would be far better if you did not hear it at all." After this stern kibosh on free expression, the meeting began.

In meetings at Murdock's the chair reads from the Big Book and calls on people to share in the order in which they arrived. The chair person does not comment on what is said, offer advice, or tell his or her own story. It was an AA meeting, not a conversation.

As people shared at Murdock's I heard about men and women who drank like I did—people who drank themselves to poverty, despair, and the brink of suicide. They were drunks like me, people who drank because they liked getting drunk. They didn't drink because of peer pressure or job stress. They drank because they liked the effect of alcohol and they drank until they couldn't stop drinking. Yet most the regulars had years of sobriety. The rookies at Murdock's had five years. The old timers boasted ten, fifteen, even twenty years of continuous sobriety. In their eyes, I with my twenty-nine days sober, was still drunk.

Meetings were ninety minutes long. During the preliminaries those with fewer than thirty days sobriety were asked to raise a hand and give a first name. At my first meeting I dutifully raised my hand and revealed my twenty-nine days without a drink. Later in the meeting I was called on to share. I said I was alcoholic, that I'd just gotten out of treatment, and that I wanted to stay sober. When I stopped speaking, the chairperson moved to the next person without comment. My announcement created nary a ripple in the Murdock's pond. Newcomers come and go there. Some leave to drink again. Others find easier groups. A few stay and get sober. For the regulars it was of no consequence either way. The door was an entrance and an exit. You didn't hurt anyone's feelings or make anyone's day by using it.

I spent that first meeting fighting back tears. Each of the stories I heard could have been my own. I wasn't crying for the person telling it, I cried for myself. At the end of that first meeting I stayed in my chair watching people clean ashtrays and wash coffee cups. When I finally stood to leave a woman approached me, grasped my hand and said, "Welcome home. We've been waiting for you." I muttered something and felt I should know her from somewhere. I begged out of any further conversation and went home. Back at the apartment I felt and then knew that Murdock's had chosen me.

I was learning how to live all over again. At the Manor I'd had the bell. The bell told me what to do, where to do it, and when to stop. I'd gotten good at the bell. There was no bell in the apartment, nothing to signify the divisions in the day. Released from the necessity of vomiting every morning I began to eat breakfast on my own. After breakfast, because I didn't have a lecture or group, I'd get a newspaper or watch a morning talk show on TV. Occasionally, I'd scan the help wanted ads for an employer in need of an unem-ployed newly sober ex-attorney. At noon I'd go to Murdock's.

I became comfortable speaking at Murdock's. When asked to share, I'd fill in the regulars about my delightfully sober morning or whine to them about the troubles from my past that insisted on reappearing. The listeners were always tolerant and impassive. For the moment all that counted was time; one day upon another without booze or drugs.

Kentucky Ken, one of the old timers at Murdock's, was a sometime spiritual leader for the group and a mentor for the newer members. He spoke in the cadences of a gospel preacher, but his message was sobriety, humility, and the twelve steps contained in the Big Book. Although Murdock's didn't abide the concept of AA sponsors—"the group is your sponsor" was the standard comment to someone seeking sponsorship—Kentucky Ken became my guide to the steps. He was always there, ready to be summoned into the small back room where the telephone took incoming calls but refused to let anyone dial out. In the privacy of the back room he bellowed out advice to newcomers and old timers alike in a voice that carried through the walls to the meeting.

I called Kentucky Ken to the back room one day to ask about step six. I'd done my step four, writing out my character defects. I'd admitted those defects to Sky Pilot in step five. Then the Manor kicked me out. Step six said we "were entirely ready to have God remove all those defects of character." I asked Ken how I was supposed to get ready. He was offended by the question.

"There's nothing to do in step six," he bellowed. "Read the book. It says we were ready. It doesn't say to do anything. Have you done step one?"

"Yes," I said. "I am powerless over alcohol."

"Step two?"

"I believe that a power greater than myself can restore me to sanity."

"What is that power?"

"For me, it is the group here. In treatment, it was the group there. . . ."

"Screw the people in treatment," he said. "They're gone. If you can't accept anything better, use the group consciousness here. Do you believe you can stay sober by coming here?"

"Yes."

"Step three?"

"I've turned my life and my will over to my higher power."

"And do you come here every day?"

"I do."

"And you carry what you learn here into the rest of your life?"

"I do."

"Step four?"

"I did it in treatment."

"Step five?"

"I did it."

"After step five did you feel at peace with yourself? Were your fears removed?" I recalled the emptiness I felt sitting on the picnic table at the Manor.

"Yes."

Ken grabbed the Big Book and stabbed at the pages with his finger. "After today's meeting go home and review each of the steps you've done. If you can honestly say you have done each one thoroughly, you are at step six. It's all in the book, but you have to read it."

"Okay," I winced.

Murdock's took the hard cases, and although I hadn't come from prison or the nut house, I considered myself one of the hard cases. By Murdock's standards I'd been an average drinker. I'd drunk more than some and less than others, but in the realm of self will I was one of the hard core. At the Manor I had turned my life over to the bell. Once out, I turned it over to Murdock's.

Despite Murdock's, my old self remained close at hand. Given half a chance, I could again start believing my own conclusions. Believing in myself and the correctness of my own deductions was harmless when limited to decisions such as crossing streets at green lights, however, I was equally capable of concluding that a drink was absolutely the best thing to top off a Sunday afternoon. From there I was only a step away from pissing my pants and blaming society for making me do it. I didn't crave liquor in the sense one craves a cigarette or a candy bar. I didn't live with an urge to drink. I simply had a mind that, after reviewing all the evidence, could conclude that having a drink was the most logical and rational thing to do at the moment. Murdock's, a bunch of hard core drunks reminding each other what it had been like with the booze, kept that insanity at bay. A reprieve was all I asked.

The Lemmings, my long time social group, slipped away from me. We continued to gather to watch football games or share a meal, but I arrived late and left early. I seldom put in an appearance at Taps. For the Lemmings, as it had been for me, drinking was a recreation in its own right. They might watch football, play golf, or shoot pool while doing it, but despite outward appearance, football and pool were condiments to the main dish of getting drunk. I was nibbling the appetizer without sharing in the meal. It left me hungry and the Lemmings slighted. I saw them less and less.

Every day at noon I returned to Murdock's for a dose of the Big Book. At Murdock's I could mingle with the alcoholics but didn't have to endure the drinking. The crowd there was a cross section of urban decay. We had a few homeless who showed up for the free coffee and a ninety-minute respite from the rain. We had doctors and lawyers, men who parked new cars outside the door and spoke in the cadence of a college education. In between were the bus drivers, cooks, and junk men who make life interesting. Our professions differed and so did our drinking. I'd been a maintenance drinker. I drank every day to stay normal. Others had been bingers. They could stay sober for weeks, even months at a time, but when they drank they drank to oblivion. The funniest stories came from the blackout drinkers, those who could start drinking in San Diego and wake up in Kansas City. Despite the differences in our personal stories and our drinking habits, we all shared two things: each of us had been alcoholic since our first drink, and none of us could ever drink like a normal person.

For the first few weeks, Murdock's was my substitute drug. The room was as comfortable and private as the bars had ever been. The meetings were stimulating and calming at the same time, and after a meeting, the day to day struggles with food, rent, and family seemed a small burden to pay for the simple joy of being sober. Each day the effect of a meeting would slowly wear off in the face of bills, job applications, and the normal frustrations of life, but Murdock's had four meetings a day. Peace was always close at hand. It was a replacement addiction, but it was safe, free, and legal.

Almost imperceptibly, I began to recover. The process was slow. A person does not recover from twenty years of drinking by spending three weeks at a musty Edwardian spa, however the human body is remarkably resilient, and I had done no truly permanent damage. I began to read again. I kept drawing, as I had at the Manor. My fear of the future became manageable.

20

I got my first pair of glasses when I was in the seventh grade. My parents bought them for me because I was having a hard time at school seeing what was written on the blackboard. When I got glasses, I could see clearly again. I could see the individual leaves on trees. I could read traffic signs a block away. My new way of seeing the world was so exciting that I became convinced I could see better than any of my friends.

"I can see the ridges on that little insulator where the electric wire attaches to the pole," I told my friend Peeve.

"I can see that too," Peeve said.

"I can see those two bees over there in the hollyhocks."

"I can see them too," Peeve said.

I was sure Peeve was lying. He hadn't gotten new glasses. How could he claim to see as well as I could?

I wore my early sobriety like I'd worn my new glasses. I felt as if I saw the world more clearly than other people, as if the minutes of my days were richer than the minutes of theirs. After all, I'd been in the valley of death and managed to emerge on the other side. Didn't that make me wiser and more appreciative of the world than people who hadn't made that journey?

My smugness was reinforced at Murdock's. There I met people who wore the same glasses and had survived the same disaster. Despite our ragged meeting hall and high unemployment rate, it was difficult when attending Murdock's not to feel just a bit superior to the rest of the world. The drinking had stopped, but the self-centeredness remained.

The immediate victim of my new sainthood was Isol. She had stopped drinking and drugging without the aid of licensed professionals. She hadn't taken the steps, she just quit. She had worked her job and paid the rent while I had contemplated the meaning of life at the Manor. She didn't read the Big Book. She didn't go to Murdock's, and she didn't lounge around admiring the world through new spiritual glasses.

Once sober, our lives took a turn for the better. The elephant in the living room was gone. For years the drinking and drug use was something we had to hide from the outside. The cans and bottles had to be cleaned up lest anyone know how much we consumed. Social dates had to be carefully planned or avoided so they wouldn't conflict with our drinking. Family and neighbors had to be kept at bay lest the truth come out. When the drinking stopped so did the hiding. People could stop by any time of the day or night.

Isol and I stopped fighting. The horrendous brawls which used to punctuate our weekends were a thing of the past. We stopped stabbing each other with those drug-enhanced insults that cut to the bone and ached for days afterward.

For a while, I told Isol everything that happened at Murdock's, but after a few weeks that stopped. I wanted her to be comfortable with my program, but it seemed she was most at ease when I kept quiet about it. At Murdock's I talked about alcohol, sobriety, honesty,

and God. At home I talked about anything except what
went on at Murdock's

Isol understood that I had to attend AA meetings.
She lived with my Big Book in the living room, but she
wasn't truly privy to what was happening inside me.
Similarly, I was much too enthralled with the changes
happening within to give much thought to how she was
surviving without the help of drugs or the program. In
a sense we were each making peace with the world but
had not yet made peace with each other.

The friends I made at the Manor dispersed and
disappeared as quickly as summer camp romances.
Once in while I would get a call from one of them,
usually seeking legal advice, and while we talked I
would get bits of gossip about how people were doing.
Rollo and some of the other Barracudas had gotten
loaded within days of being released. A small social
group had developed in which the members justified
their continued drug use by the wrongs inflicted upon
them at the Manor. My fantasy of us all remaining
clean was not to be.

Daniel had stayed straight and was back to teaching
school. On the phone he extolled the virtues of the
atheist AA group that Wayne had mentioned. They did
the Big Book without God and apparently had a good
time doing it. Daniel was making a tour of Portland AA.
He'd seen Big John at the waterfront and had gone out
to the suburbs to attend a meeting with Stevie. I made
arrangements for him to meet me at Murdock's for one
of the five thirty meetings.

On becoming a regular at Murdock's, I'd adopted

the official group opinion that Murdock's was somehow just a little better than any other AA group in town. The arrogance that plagues alcoholics is not limited to individuals; it shows up in the personalities of groups as well. With Daniel sitting across the table from me, however, our little den of spirituality seemed shabbier and more removed from the world than usual. The duals, people who had stacked alcoholism on top of schizophrenia or depression, were out in force that day. AA kept them sober but had little impact on the mental illness. They embarrassed me in front of Daniel.

On the day of Daniel's visit, the sharing seemed to center on God and jobs, two things I still didn't have. According to the unwritten Murdock's tradition, people in meetings attributed their sobriety to "my higher power, who I choose to call God." The phrase, I suppose, was to show tolerance for people like my old C.A., Pixie Patty, who might still have a chicken for a higher power, but the reference always reminded me of my unresolved God problem. The subject of jobs wasn't much better. Daniel was back teaching school, drawing a fair salary and diligently building his retirement fund. I, with all my degrees, and now sober, was still as unemployed as I'd been when drinking.

After the meeting, Daniel and I went across the street for coffee. As it turned out he had enjoyed Murdock's, warts and all.

"I like the emphasis on the Big Book," he said, "I need more of that. I don't read it much anymore."

"Well, there's no lack of Big Book at Murdock's." I told him. "It's like that every time, but sometimes the group is a little more, how should I say it, normal."

"They're fine," he said. "If we were well adjusted we wouldn't need any of this."

"How's Big John?" I asked.

"I had dinner with him last week," Daniel said. "He's a book thumper again, preaching the gospel of AA."

"And Stevie?"

"She's fine," he said, "She started her own group, just like we predicted. She got sick of the group close to her. Now she has about ten people coming over to her house twice a week. I went once. She was the chairman and everyone had a good time. She is a housewife now—quit real estate all together."

"And how are you?" I asked.

"Fine, I guess. I still have the craving. The groups help when I go, but it's still a day to day battle. How about you? Has God removed the desire to drink?"

"I don't have the urge much, but I go to Murdock's every day. I haven't met God there, but I don't want to walk in there and raise my hand again for having less than thirty days."

"If God doesn't work, peer pressure will?"

"Hey, peer pressure didn't start me drinking, but it has done just fine at keeping me sober."

"How's the job search going?" he asked.

"I'm still looking."

My search for employment was the major disaster in my new sobriety. The law schools were churning out bright energetic graduates by the thousands to fill the few openings in an overcrowded profession. The entry-level positions belonged to them. Employers looking for experience weren't impressed by a middle-aged man who'd taken a three-year sabbatical to study the effects of alcohol on himself.

In the first months of sobriety, when attending meetings, I often had the feeling that every comment was aimed directly at me. When Kentucky Ken told his story of coming off the streets with an attitude, sipping coffee at AA meetings for months, unemployed and broke, his story turned the AA coffee in my mouth to mud. "Work or die," he would yell, and I would cringe in my chair.

During the day I applied for jobs at gas stations and delivery services. In the evenings I worked on getting reinstated to the Bar. I considered the Oregon Bar Association a collection of overpaid busybodies, but I needed the Bar's stamp of approval if I were ever to practice law again. I did enough home study to satisfy my continuing legal education requirements and then took a revolutionary new approach to dealing with bureaucrats. I told the truth. I explained to them that I'd quit paying Bar dues and malpractice insurance because I needed the money for booze. I told them about the trip to Malady Manor and about Murdock's. They accepted my reinstatement application as well as my money and said they'd think about it.

I spent my days waiting. I waited for phone calls about jobs. I waited for phone calls from the Bar. I waited for someone to tell me what to do with the rest of my life. Once I'd been close to capsizing in the storm of life. In the first months of sobriety I became becalmed. I had nothing to do or say, nothing to offer either an employer or the world. I existed, but I had no goals and no point to my days.

On Wednesday evenings I was supposed to attend the continuing care program at the Manor. Isol and I went together. She would attend an Alanon meeting where people learned how to live with alcoholics while I attended group with a bunch of Manor alumni. The alumni meetings were stiff and uncomfortable. We would gather in one of the first floor rooms and sit on the good furniture. Each week a different counselor ran the show, and in turn we would be asked to tell the group our experience that week without alcohol. Once a person had told his tale of woe the other patients were permitted to comment, criticize, and offer advice. At Murdock's cross talk—comment on what someone else had said—was strictly prohibited. At aftercare it was encouraged. I didn't see the point in what we did. Addicts don't take advice. Straight people may never understand that, but other addicts should.

After a month of aftercare I stopped going. I'd paid my five grand for an introduction to AA and once Murdock's had chosen me, the Manor seemed super-fluous. Isol's experience was equally unsatisfying. She met people at the Alanon meetings who had known what it was like to live with a drinker, but the people there hadn't gotten drunk with him. Lots of wives had poured liquor down the sink so their husbands would-n't drink it. Isol had poured it down her throat.

"Those women got mad at their husbands," she told me, "I got drunk at you."

Shortly after we stopped going to aftercare I received notice in the mail that the Manor was closing. Residential treatment was going out of style and the insurance companies were refusing to pay for it. With outpatient treatment becoming the wave of the future, a castle full of dormitory rooms had little chance. A conglomerate of spiritually starved Buddhists had made an offer on the building to use it as a meditation center, and the Manor management had capitulated to economic reality.

I felt sad about the closing of the Manor. Almost everyone at Murdock's had been to one or more treatment centers. The treatments seldom worked, and most of the people who'd been through them ended up resenting the people who'd failed to cure them. The answer, they asserted, was AA, God and the seats at Murdock's. Insurance-sucking social workers and pop psychologists were not going to change that. I never resented the Manor. All in all, it had given me a fair start on sobriety, and even though the address to my first AA meeting had cost Isol's insurance company several thousand dollars, I was better off with the address than without it.

My days took on a comfortable sameness. I woke early and read the Big Book, took Isol to work, and searched for a job. I went to Murdock's at noon, took care of household chores, cooked dinner, read in the evening, and went to bed early. I collected time.

One evening in my third month of sobriety I was reading a novel in my bathrobe when the phone rang.

"This is Robert," the caller said.

"Robert?"

"From the Manor," he said, "I was your roommate."

"Oh, Robert," I remembered. "What's up?"

"I'm in town," he said, "not far from you. I've been staying with a friend and I just had to get out of there. I've been drunk for four days."

It was not what I wanted to hear. AA emphasized that we are always on call to help the alcoholic who still suffers, but I figured that if I didn't call them they wouldn't call me. Besides, I was only three months sober myself, still nursing a hangover by Murdock's standards. I had nothing to offer and no inclination to ruin a nice evening by talking to a drunk who I'd never liked all that much when sober.

"Where are you?" I asked. He told me, and unfortunately it was not so far that I couldn't be there within a few minutes. I hung up my bathrobe, dressed, and tried to think of what I ought to say to him. Isol was not pleased with the interruption but offered to let him in and keep the coffee flowing as long as she didn't have to say anything. I started up my truck and headed into the night.

I found Robert at a bus stop bench about a mile from my apartment. He was sweating alcohol, and as soon as he got in the truck, the cab reeked of beer.

"How long have you been in Portland?" I asked.

"Two months now," he told me. "I had problems at home so I took a job here."

"Do you have a place?"

"I'm staying with this guy I know. He's on unemployment. He drinks all day, every day. He doesn't have a problem with it, but I started drinking with him. Other stuff too. I had to get away from there for a while." Robert was at the end, or maybe in the middle of a long slow drunk. His words weren't slurred; he wasn't gregarious or depressed. He was tired—too tired to sleep and too drunk to wake up.

At the apartment Isol had the coffee poured. I was embarrassed bringing him to my home. His family had money, and despite his addictions, he was used to more elaborate housing than my cluttered apartment. As he sipped coffee I rummaged through my knowledge of the Big Book and my experiences at Murdock's for directions on dealing with an active drunk. I came up blank. Supposedly, I should have been able to communicate with him because we shared the disease, but as I sat across the coffee table from him, it seemed we had nothing in common. He was drunk and I was sober. I remembered how it had been, but I couldn't feel it enough to reach back. After some strained chit chat he broke the ice.

"How did you do it?" he asked me. "You had the bug as bad as I do."

"I've tried to stay with the program," I said.

"Did you go to AA meetings and all that?"

"I go every day."

"I tried," he said. "At first I went to a couple meetings, but they just made me want to get high. The people there were pathetic. They were all losers. All I could think was that they should get out of there and get a life."

I'd been away from the arrogance of drunkenness

and had started to forget. My anger flared. He was drunk, not them. Who here was the loser?

"I follow the Big Book and go to meetings," I said. "At first I didn't like the meetings, but now I like going."

"I can't go to them," he stated flatly. "At the first one I was so bored I poured out a packet of Nutrasweet on the table and scraped the powder into little lines on the table. They thought I was weird, but hearing all that stuff made me crazy. I have to do it another way."

I had another way for him. Go out and drink for another ten years. Drink yourself into destitution, depression, and into the shadow of death. Lose everything you ever had and then drink more until you're at the edge of suicide, to the place where it's sobriety or death. Then you can go to AA or the grave. Either way, you will stop drinking. That was my program. Go ahead, do it the way I did.

Instead of yelling I told him to read the Big Book, but I could tell as I said it that it wasn't the right thing. "I didn't get it at first," I said. "If you are doing what it says the meetings won't bother you." I proceeded to remind him of the lowlights of my own story, emphasizing his youth and the opportunity to avoid my mistakes. "The craving goes away," I said. "My hours are not filled with fighting the urge to drink. I have peace to make with those I harmed, and with God, but I am comfortable being straight."

"I don't believe in God," he said, "I happen to know that you don't either." He was right, in a sense, but I understood that my beliefs didn't matter much. Life was not going to conform to my perception of it. In his drunkenness Robert was making the world over with his mind. "I'm making good money now."

"Good," I said, "but it won't matter if you are drunk."

"Money always matters."

"You're sleeping in a spare room of an unemployed alcoholic. What good is your money? It just lets you keep up the same shit for another day. Come to a meeting with me in the morning. Try my group."

"Okay," he said. I was surprised he agreed.

"Stay here tonight. We'll go to the six thirty meeting in the morning."

"I have to go back. I can't stay."

"Stay," I said.

"No. I have to go back."

We had another cup of coffee and I drove Robert back to his friend's apartment. He was a no-show at Murdock's the next morning, and I never heard from him again.

The evening with Robert left me angry for several days. Despite all I had learned in my journey through the disease, I could not stop myself from blaming Robert for his illness. Alcoholism was still for me a carousel of blame and anger. Robert was not as he should be. He was addicted to alcohol and cocaine. The fact that he wouldn't and I couldn't change that made me angry. My first few months of sobriety were the happiest times I had had in years, but in true alcoholic style, I was always prepared to give away the reins to my happiness to the sickest person who happened to walk through my life.

A day after the visit from Robert, I got a job. A company hired me to work graveyard shift inventorying department and grocery stores. The work was a long way from practicing law, but it was work, and I threw myself into it with all my sober vigor. Isol was elated. I didn't make much money, but it was more than I made unemployed. The important thing was that I was once again useful to others. The certificate of appreciation was a paycheck.

Working in sobriety was entirely different. For years, work had been the daily discomfort I had endured so I would have a ticket through the tavern door. Work was the road, but never the destination. When I no longer had anywhere to go, that changed. Work was the end in itself. By societal standards the work was hard and the hours long, but that is the case only if there is some place else you need to be. I just wanted to participate. I gave my paychecks to Isol, taking my satisfaction from the feeling of exhaustion at the end of the shift. For the first time, the process was the result. I realized why Kentucky Ken yelled "work or die." Work was life.

21

I discovered God on a cross-town bus. Or maybe it was God who found me. Up to the time of meeting God, the day had been uneventful. I was off work and had spent most of the morning in the law library. I'd done some shopping and was returning home for a late lunch. The bus was rattling across one of the bridges that span the Willamette River when, all of a sudden, I found God.

As I looked up from my newspaper at the river, the city colors had transformed. Both inside and outside of the bus, objects had assumed rich and vibrant versions of their normal hues. Things around me, rather than merely reflecting ambient light in that portion of the spectrum that makes them appear red or blue, seemed to be emitting light—glowing if you will—with the beautiful mysteriousness of a cloud laying across the full moon. The sounds of the bus, the chatting passengers, and the traffic noises outside had fused, and what had once been an everyday urban cacophony was an undulating orchestration harmonizing with the colors. The sounds on the bus made no music in the human sense, but seemed to rise and fall according to a score written by nature, as the sound of waves is the music of the seashore. My first reaction was to check the faces of my fellow passengers for signs of alarm or astonishment. Facing an earthquake or a car accident, I wouldn't have hesitated to call out to them, to bring to their attention what was happening, but I was not about to leap up and yell that the colors of the world around us had changed. That sort of thing is just not acceptable on Portland busses. I kept my seat.

I felt weak at first, as if the tendons that held my joints together had gone slack. The book bag I carried felt heavy on my lap. My skin was electrically sensitive, and waves of warmth pulsed through my body as the centrifugal force of the turning bus pushed me against the sunlit window. I sat very still, awed by what was happening, and repeated to myself the AA phrase "this too shall pass."

The sensations did not pass away. I ruled out the possibility of a flashback from a bygone LSD trip or a temporary imbalance in my chemical make-up. After the initial shock I relaxed and watched as everything around me became beautiful.

The blue Oregon sky stretched over the sprawling city to Mount Hood in the distance. The heating pad warmth of the summer day brought up from inside me a deep sense that form had emerged from chaos. The discordant fragments of experience and sensation that make up life in the city fell together. The jigsaw puzzle was for a moment complete and I was permitted to look upon it. I saw and felt order around me—I saw purpose in the world, and I felt my place in it.

The bus arrived at my stop. The trees in the neighborhood were greener than they had ever been. Each house on the street was perfect. I—despite my drinking, my failures, and my night job—was exactly where I was meant to be. Everything in my past had been absolutely necessary for the world to be as it was that day, and on that walk home the world was in harmony. I could not and would not be other than what I was.

If true humility be the absence of pride, then, for a few hours, I was humble. I was relieved of the burden of self. I was humble before a power, an experience, a feeling, so extraordinary, that I seemed to lose my sense of self all together. I was a mass of whirling atoms moving through the neighborhood, qualitatively no different from any other conglomeration of basic elements, but absolutely crucial to the universe, for without my presence on that street the design would be askew. I could play my part and no other.

When I arrived at my apartment I went out on our small deck to think, but rather than contemplating and concluding in any rational sense, I became filled with the knowledge that what was happening to me was God. God, for whatever reason, if God uses reason, was making himself known to me. In a moment, the discussions, the theology, and the intellectual inquiries were swept away. The unanswerable questions—Can God make a rock so big he can't move it? Why do bad things happen to good people?—simply evaporated. They weren't answered; they vanished. I had a glimpse of a truth that made the questions irrelevant. My years of melancholy cynicism crumbled in a few hours.

I had often snidely asserted that I would believe in God if he would just step on down from heaven and make his presence known to me. I said that with the firm expectation that that it could not happen. And then it did. My years of active atheism were over in a day, ending as I physically experienced the presence of

God around me. Without my consent, I had been changed.

In the following days my sense of God's presence waned, and my world returned to normal under the weight of the mundane. The rent still came due, and meals still had to be cooked. The colors and sounds of the world returned to what they were, but the memory of what had happened was burned into my being.

That day the very nature of my existence changed. I had always existed in a dark place. I had eyes so I could look outside the dark place and see the world around me. I had senses so I could hear the world, smell odors, and feel the textures of nature. If I broke a bone I felt pain; if I exercised I became tired and slept. However, no part of the world ever came into the dark place. I couldn't see inside the dark place, but I was sure that I was alone there. That was how life had always been and how I expected it always to be.

I couldn't furnish the dark place with objects as one might furnish a house, so I furnished it with thoughts, memories, and fantasies. Those were my inside playthings. I'd read Moby Dick when I was in college. I no longer had the book but I kept Captain Ahab and the white whale in my dark place and could play with them whenever I wanted. I'd walked across the Golden Gate Bridge when I was twenty-two, and I could return there in memory whenever I had the urge. I had literature, history, and philosophy with which I could construct thought machines that would scuttle across the floor of the dark place. I could build them, take them apart, and build them again. But despite the thought toys I kept there, I was there alone.

I had always had an address, and a telephone number. People could send me letters, call me, or talk to me on the street, but no one ever came inside the dark place. No one could look through the same eye holes that I looked through or play with the same thought toys that I played with. No one could see in there, or see what I saw from there.

Other people made me lonely. They mystified me. Did they live in their own dark places? What kind of toys did they play with? Did colors look the same to them as they did to me? All I could see from my hiding place were the shells of people. Maybe they had no more substance than the light on a movie screen. The thought toys I kept in the dark place couldn't answer my questions about them and couldn't relieve the loneliness.

Inside the dark place I was decaying. Alone in there, I had tuned mean and ugly. As a child I did not want to be a liar, yet I lied and became one. I did not want to be a thief and a cheat, but I stole and I conned. I did not want to be a drunk and an addict, but I drank and I used. With each of these acts, I decayed. Alone in the dark place I became an ogre that had to stay hidden from the world. When I drank I could forget that I was an ogre, that I was a liar and a thief, and that I was decaying. Once sober and free of drugs I felt the decay and the ugliness anew. I felt the pain and the loneliness of the guilty.

After that day on the bus, things were different in the dark place. Someone else was inside with me. The other saw what I saw. It knew the things I had done. It had experienced my life beside me. It was other, but it understood what it felt like to be me.

I tried to see the other, but no light comes into the dark place. I could only sense his presence, vaguely hear his movements, and feel his thoughts. He had experienced the lives of many people before me, and when he brushed against me as he moved about the dark place he put me in communion with all the others who walk upon this earth. When I seek him and he answers he lets me be one of many, and I am no longer alone.

The other being in the box felt the pain I felt. He bore with me the guilt of my lies, my stealing and my addiction. He shed tears with me, and when he touched me my pain was relieved. He knew that I didn't mean to hurt those I had hurt. He did not remove my sins, but he shared them and he understood what it means to sin. In the sharing, my guilt became bearable. He was free of sin, and when he touched me I had a glimpse of that freedom. There was a promise in his touch, a promise that I might sin no more.

In the days that followed my bus ride I felt that my decay had stopped. I was not alone, and being loved, loving others was suddenly possible. I would do no evil today.

22

Discovering God causes a practicing atheist a variety of practical difficulties. First, he has to decide whether he wants to keep God around. God may show up unexpectedly, but doesn't hang around where he's not wanted. Second, the atheist has to decide who to tell about God. A wrong step here has the potential for serious social embarrassment. And, finally, if he decides to keep God, he's got to decide what, if anything he plans to do with God. Slippery places and unexpected pitfalls abound.

In the first few days of my relationship with God— after the drama of the day on the bus was over—I carried God around cupped in my hands, much as a child would carry a bird that had fallen from its nest. I wanted to protect God, hold him gingerly and love him. Spirituality seemed to me a fragile thing, and each morning upon waking I would reach for it quickly, as I did my glasses, to make sure it hadn't disappeared in the night.

In the evenings, before going to sleep, I prayed. Prayer was no longer the awkward thing it had been in the basement of the Manor. I followed the directions in the Big Book. I reviewed my day, admitting where I'd gone wrong and asking for the strength to right the wrongs. I asked for direction. I didn't pray for myself; I simply asked God to reveal his will for me and to give me the strength to carry it out. That was how the Big Book said to do it, and for me, it worked.

Despite my change of belief, I was apprehensive about taking any actual directions from God. I was afraid that God might tell me to dress funny and preach the gospel on street corners. He might order me to give my money to poor people or travel to some place where they didn't speak English. I didn't want to become a religious nut. God eventually put me at ease about these worries. He didn't actually talk to me, but he somehow made me understand that after a whole week of spirituality, I was not high on the list of people destined to receive a calling. For the time being, spreading the word would be left up to those with a bit more experience.

For a while I kept God a secret. As far as anyone knew I was the same irreverent atheist I had always been—an alcoholic atheist, an AA atheist, but an atheist nevertheless. My problem with telling anyone about the change stemmed from my loudly-held opinion that believers in God were nuts. No matter how sincere or well intentioned, when push came to shove, they were just a little bit touched in the head. Becoming one of them was not an easy thing for me to share with others.

I managed to hold it in for about two weeks, and then I told Isol. We'd spent a quiet evening together reading in our bathrobes. As bedtime neared Isol reached for the TV remote to switch on the local news. I stopped her and said I had something I had to say.

I told her what had happened on the bus. I told her about the dark place, and God getting inside of it. I told her about my prayers. I said I had changed, that I now believed. She listened to it all, and when I finished she patted me on the arm comfortingly and said, "You're nuts. I'm going to bed."

I was disappointed but not deterred by Isol's response to my tale, so I resolved to take my story to Murdock's. This took a bit of nerve. It was doctrine at Murdock's that the spiritual life was a result of doing the steps. It didn't start on a bus to a person half way through the program. I was constantly reminded at Murdock's that "Most of our experiences are what the psychologist William James calls the 'educational variety' because they develop slowly over a period of time. Quite often friends of the newcomer are aware of the difference long before he is himself." The quote from the Big Book did not apply to me. My conversion had been sudden and dramatic, and as far as I knew, none of my friends had noticed anything at all.

Despite the quote from James, I thought I might get a better reception at Murdock's than I'd gotten from Isol. The old timers at Murdock's lived the spiritual life. Unlike Isol, they had probably been through similar experiences and would be able to identify with my transformation. I thought out what I was going to say, and then, at a noon meeting with plenty of old timers present, I told them. I told them about the colors and the sounds, the feeling that the world was coming to an end, and the feeling of the presence of God inside me. I told them how it was to have my prayers listened to and how it felt when God answered them. I told it all. When I finished sharing, the room was silent, and the chairperson moved on to the next member. I awaited the end of the meeting, the time when the formalities would be over and the informal discussions begin. After the Lord's Prayer, which closed each meeting, Kentucky Ken walked over to me. "How's it going?" he asked.

"Fine," I said.

"Staying sober?"

"Yep."

"That was quite a story you told today," he said.

"It all happened."

"Wow."

"Do you think that it was—that it was the real thing?"

"I think you're nuts," he said, "but what I think doesn't matter." I was crushed, and he could see it in my face. He comforted me. "But we're all a little bit crazy here. The important thing is that you are sober."

After my experiences with Isol and at Murdock's, I once again kept quiet about God. If someone wanted to know, they could ask, and with the kind of people I knew, no one ever asked. I didn't seem to be doing God or myself any good by telling people.

I decided that my active relationship with God was a result of my working the steps. I'd read hundreds of books in my life, and many of them had dealt with God or related subjects, but while working with the Big Book, God had come to me on a bus. The two had to be related. Not wanting to lose what I had found, I gave up reading everything except the Big Book and the newspaper. Although intensely curious about what had happened to me, I was afraid of putting it under an intellectual microscope for fear that examination would kill it. Intellectualism and skepticism were tools that had gotten me nowhere. I was not about to let them screw me up again. I abandoned my rational self and nurtured the intuitive.

With nurturing, my communication with God became easy and natural. I would ask for his direction, and it would come to me. I could distinguish his help from my own thoughts, and I found doing his will much easier than I had expected. God reveled in the mundane. I would ask God what to do, and he would tell me to get up, brush my teeth, eat breakfast, and do the next thing on my agenda for the day. He got a certain amount of amusement out of the fact that I hadn't thought of these things on my own. I was embarrassed by the simplicity of the answers. He gave me the impression that I wasn't particularly bright.

God liked me to pack a healthy, but not unreasonable, amount of living into my days. He liked me to work. When my boss asked for volunteers to work overtime, God raised my hand. Although he worked me a lot of hours, I seemed to have more free time, more time to pursue hobbies and recreation, than I had ever had. I began painting and drawing again. I wrote letters. I cleaned the apartment, listened to classical music, and rode my bike. All things considered, God had some good ideas.

After my experience on the bus, the group of drunks at Murdock's was no longer my higher power. I'd found another, and as they say at Murdock's, "I chose to call him God." In theory, then, I didn't need Murdock's any more, but God was clear in his directions that I continue to attend AA meetings. For richer or poorer, in sickness and in health, I was part of Murdock's. The folks at Malady Manor had sobered me up, but AA, particularly Murdock's, was showing me how to live sober. I owed a debt for that favor and would have to repay it. Repayment meant attending the meetings and being useful to the group.

Although God spent most of his time leading me by the hand through the mundane, he did have certain commandments for me to keep. Killing, stealing, lying and pride were all prohibited. I wasn't all that surprised by this. I'd read about these prohibitions somewhere before. I'd never killed anyone, so that didn't present any major change of life-style. I wasn't in a position anymore where I could steal much, and with a modicum of effort I could resist the urge to pocket useful little items that might cross my path at work. Lying, however, was difficult to give up. I'd been lying for so many years that lies appeared fully formed in my mind and were out of my mouth before I realized what had happened. I vowed to stop, but just couldn't. In most cases they were silly lies, fabrications told to coworkers to make me appear more interesting than I really was, embellishments to the truth to lubricate my way through uncomfortable situations. When I reviewed each day in the evening before going to sleep, I never had to worry about murder. I got through most days without theft, but going a day without telling a lie was difficult. Giving up the sins I was good at was going to take some work.

When I lied I felt like I had failed in what I wanted to do that day, but there were seldom any personal consequences that flowed directly from my lying. That was not the case with pride. Pride punished me instantly. Despite my experience with God and all evidence to the contrary, I clung to the idea that I possessed certain intrinsic characteristics that set me apart from and made me better than most people. From this lofty position it was my duty to dish out blame for the things that were wrong in the world.

I liked being a judge. If someone at work left his job undone and I had to finish it, I was there to take that person's moral inventory. "If you can't finish it, don't start it," I'd proclaim to myself. That was my rule, and my rules applied to everybody. Because I was both judge and jury, every wrong I encountered during the day resulted in someone being convicted. After finding fault and establishing blame, it became my job to design a punishment. I'd vow not to be there when that person needed help, or I'd think of some little thing to do or say that would make his life just a little bit harder. It was my moral duty.

I would lay awake at night nurturing frustration at the unpunished sinners of the world. The reason for my insomnia was that my pride had been hurt. Someone had done something without considering how it might affect me. That was unforgivable, and to make things right, I was willing to torture myself into the night. God took a hike when I was healing the wounds to my own self-importance. Once I had finished dishing out punishment to sloppy coworkers, rude waiters, and in-laws who dropped in unexpectedly, he would return to remind me that I was the one who was suffering. The sinners I was judging were all sound asleep between warm sheets. I'd whine to him that I didn't want to judge people. I simply could not stop.

"Are you powerless over it?" he seemed to ask, and I would see that I was. I needed to ask for help. I would apologize for my stubbornness and ask that my sentence be commuted. I'd promise to do better in the morning, and he would put me to sleep.

God and I had been roommates for about a month when he let me know that he wasn't fragile. He wasn't going to break. Like my first meeting with him, this came to me in a flash.

I was sitting in the noon meeting at Murdock's. Although I was working long hours, I still attended three or four meetings a week. In the months since leaving the Manor I'd learned the standard phrases and was accepted as one of the regulars. "It takes what it takes to get you here. It takes what it takes to keep you here." "The door works both ways, if you don't like it here, we'll gladly refund your misery." "The answer is in the Book, it's highlighted in black." "Keep the plug in the jug." "Progress not perfection." "Easy does it."

One of the regulars who seldom came to the noon meeting began extolling the virtues of the Big Book as the answer to all life's problems, not just the problem of drink. He made the point that AA, the organization and the meetings, are named after the book. *Alcoholics Anonymous* is the book, not the meetings. All the answers were there. In fact, he said, he hadn't read anything other than the Big Book for ten years and had no intention of reading anything else before he died. I was shocked. It was the logic and rationale of ignorance. It condemned all literature and thought outside his chosen gospel. Visions of book burnings, the Inquisition, and the destruction of the library at Alexandria danced in my head.

What he had said was wrong. God did not thrive on ignorance; he hadn't given me an intellect so I could abandon it. The man who spoke may have been right for him. Maybe his life was such that if he didn't read the Big Book, he wouldn't read at all, but my ability to read and understand was the gift God had bestowed upon me. God didn't ask athletes to stop running. He didn't make singers quit music, and he didn't make worn out cross-examiners stop asking questions. I was dealing with God, not a jealous mistress.

That day at Murdock's my curiosity got its driving privileges back, and I was off and running. I had a lot of questions. Was I a certain religion? What had really happened on the bus? Had things like that happened to others? How could I be sure it was God, and not some clever servant of lower regions? Was I mentally deranged? If I was crazy, how bad was it, and was there a cure? Did I want a cure if there was one?

First I tackled the religion questions. I didn't ask God directly. I sensed that he didn't fill out surveys, and he had never given me any direction on theological issues. He had never mentioned whether there was life after death, where heaven was, or what religion, if any, I was supposed to be. God gave me clear direction when it came to brushing my teeth, but seemed to leave a lot of the philosophical matters up to me.

I started by reading the Bible. I read it in the same way that I'd read it at the Manor, not to be critical, but to be open to the message. I figured that if the book had been inspired by God, written by him so to speak, I would sense it, and I did. It did seem touched by God, or at least written by men who had been touched by God. However, I didn't find anything that made me more Christian and less something else.

I read the Koran. It too seemed inspired by God. It contained the words of a prophet, but it didn't make me feel like a Muslim. I read the *Book of Mormon* and the *Bagatavita*. I doubted that I'd been meant to be Mormon or Hindu. I reread some of the ancient gnostic gospels that had fascinated me in years past. I found them interesting, but the thought of being a gnostic in the twentieth century seemed a bit unrealistic.

Isol found my new choice of reading material to be incomprehensible. "How can you read that stuff?" she asked.

"I move my eyes across the paper," I answered.

"But it's so boring."

"I'm a lawyer," I said. "I'm trained to read boring things."

Being a lawyer, I was acutely sensitive to the amount of law in God's books. The Ten Commandments are reasonably famous. Leviticus governs details of day-to-day life down to the minutest detail. The laws in the Koran cover everything from diet to probate. The Big Book had the twelve steps.

I struggled with the question of which came first, the relationship with God or obedience to God's laws.

The law, the Ten Commandments or the Oregon statutes, had been no more than societal norms until the day on the bus. Laws had no personal connection to me, and had no intrinsic value other than keeping me out of jail, and deterring others from stealing my car. However, I hadn't had a personal experience with God until I'd made an honest effort to follow directions for living set out in the Big Book. Had obedience led me to God, or did God show me the value in obedience? The chicken and the egg came to mind.

My religious readings didn't lead me to a specific religion. It wasn't that I couldn't accept any of them, but rather that I couldn't reject any of them. Being a Christian, presumably, prevents one from being a Muslim. I found as much God in the Koran as I did in the Bible. God himself seemed amused by my efforts and limited his guidance to reminding me that I should not let my reading make me late for work.

Although I was in no sense disappointed by my journey through God's library, I eventually turned my efforts to more earthly matters. The changes I had experienced corresponded in time to what had happened at the Manor and at Murdock's. I read about the origin of AA. The story of how a drunk lawyer, a drunk proctologist and a bunch of moral idealists found a way to combat alcoholism makes for interesting and humorous reading.

Conventional wisdom down at Murdock's was that AA and the twelve steps to recovery was a miracle in which the answer for the alcoholic had emerged whole from the foreheads of the first one hundred members, much as Hephestus sprang from the brow of Hera. I was disconcerted to discover that much of the Big Book had been lifted from the philosophical and psychological writings of William James. His book, *The Varieties of Religious Experience*, had been at Bill W.'s side as the Big Book was written. In it was the science of religion.

Reading James made me feel normal. What had happened to me had not been supernatural in any spooky sense. It had not even been unusual. I had converted. People do it all the time. James described my experience exactly. Trepidation and fear had evaporated and I had a renewed "willingness to be" even though my outward circumstances remained the same. I sensed truths not known to me before, and the world about me appeared to have undergone an objective change. Newness and beauty had settled upon it. These were the elements of the change from skepticism to belief. I had experienced each one of them.

God had taken up residence within me. For me, God consciousness was like living with a hamster in my pants. Sometimes the beast was warm and cuddly, sometimes annoying, but it was always there, and with the hamster I would never be alone again. People had been going through the change for thousands of years. Moses had a hamster in his pants too. The phenomenon was no more unusual than teen rebellion and middle aged pouch. No matter what Isol said or how they felt down a Murdock's, I wasn't nuts.

If I fit the James's stereotype, the change that began on the bus would be the most important thing that would ever happened to me. The discordant pieces of the universe had come together and become the symphony of life rather than the drudgery of survival. I felt repose, the comfortable feeling that no matter what had happened at work or around the apartment, all was right with the world; everything was as it was supposed to be. What I'd received was a gift that couldn't be bought or sold; it could be thrown away but never stolen.

Although the religious experience has incalculable value to the person experiencing it, I had my doubts about its practical impact. My conversion occurred at a time when TV evangelists were sitting in jails, priests were child molesters, and religious wars were fermenting around the world.

I wondered what my conversion meant for the world around me. On the personal level, I turned my life over to God, asking his direction and the strength to carry it out. The jobs I was assigned seemed to have social value. I was supposed to work, be helpful to others, stay out of the judging business, and tell the truth. Each of these behaviors has a certain social utility, however I couldn't guarantee anyone that on the morrow I wouldn't be ordered by God into a holy war against convenience stores or some other cosmic malefactor. My faith was above and separate from my contract with society. Many strange things have been done in the name of God. I hadn't done any of them, but in putting my reliance on him, I couldn't guarantee that I wouldn't.

As an atheist I'd spent a lot of time pondering the

social utility of religion. Was mankind evolving beyond it? Was it the opiate of the masses? With God in my pants, those matters seemed less important. The religious experience was not a social issue. To the social scientists, tied by funding and technology to the aims of government, it might look dangerous, and in the academic world, spirituality might seem outlandish, but for the person who experiences it, God makes true individuality possible.

I put my volume of James on my bookshelf. This was no easy task, because, for years, as a hedge against excessive pomposity, I had limited myself to owning no more than six feet of books. Thus, every time I kept a book that I'd read, something had to go. A Marquez novel and a titillating history by Procopius bit the dust. James went between my Bible and the Big Book. My previous difficulties over inconsistencies between science and God were gone. The conflict between the two had not been resolved; it just didn't matter any more.

My journey from Genesis to James was a fun road trip. Like a trip to Mecca, everyone should try it once. However, I didn't learn any heretofore unknown universal truths worth putting in the newspaper. I didn't find out if there is life after death or what religion is the true religion. On occasions the sensations I had felt on the bus would return, but they seldom lasted for more than a few minutes before disappearing. Most days, I simply trudged the road in front of me. I worked, ate, and tried to be a good husband to

Isol. I'd had a spiritual experience. Each day I had chance to live a spiritual life.

23

The seventh step required me to humbly ask God to remove my defects of character. The Big Book provides a simple prayer for this step, but being a stalwart opponent of anything simple, I made as big a production out of it as I could. I planned the event for a day when I was off and Isol was working. I selected a public park close to my apartment as the proper venue. The park had the trees and ponds so often associated with spiritual things, but it was still a part of the city.

On the day of the blessed event I grabbed my Big Book and took a bus to the park. Busses were good luck for me in spiritual matters. For a while I sat in front of the duck pond, contemplating what I was about to do. I wondered what I would be like without my defects in character. They seemed to define me. The lies, the pride, the self-righteousness that often reached to pomposity seemed to be who I was. They were the things that made other people notice me. I was concerned that without them I might become invisible. "The squeaky wheel gets the grease," my dad used to say. I liked getting the grease.

I left the duck pond and went up on a grassy hill where I could look down upon mothers pushing their strollers next to the water. I said the Serenity Prayer and the Lord's Prayer. Then I prayed personally and earnestly. I reviewed my faults, remembered the damage I had done, and asked God to take my faults from me. In closing I read the seventh step prayer from the Big Book, making the words my own as I read. As humbly as I could I asked God to remove my defects.

My prayer was answered almost immediately. The answer was "No."

I walked down from the hill with the same defects of character I had taken up there, but I didn't feel let down about the answer. My most glaring defects no longer controlled me anyway. I hadn't lied to anyone for a couple of days. I hadn't gotten drunk or stoned for close to a year. I spent very little time dwelling on what was wrong with other people or the world in general. Even my self-centeredness, that firm belief in the correctness of my own opinions, was becoming manageable. I occasionally thought of others and once in a while I was useful. I was becoming normal.

Life at Murdock's followed the traditions. The meetings were the same day after day, and I attended as often as work allowed. The meetings gave me a sense of order and repose that is scarce in the work-a-day world. None of life's problems were particularly vexing when compared to the problems I had escaped. When agitated, a trip to Murdock's put everything in perspective.

One day at Murdock's I was sitting at one of the tables drawing cartoons while a young man just out of treatment was sharing about his difficulties coming up with ways to have fun in sobriety. All drunks experience the same problem. The young man was speaking in alcoholic code. He was really wondering how he was going to get the thrill of the high, get out of his head and escape to the zone, without booze or drugs. It had nothing to do with fun. Fun was the code word for those long wasted hours that he used to spend drunk, hours that now loomed empty in front of him. He missed the danger, the uncertainty, and the distortion of time. If he managed to stay sober for a few months the hours would fill themselves, and he would wonder why he had even considered it a problem. I looked up from my drawing in the middle of his talk. Someone had arrived late to the meeting. It was Tess.

I hadn't seen anyone from the Manor for months, and suddenly Tess, the archfiend and confiscator of golf clubs, was sitting at the table next to me. Her presence made me ill at ease, as if the teacher had just walked in on a student bull session. I felt as if the bell had rung, and I hadn't gone to the right room. She noticed me, and nodded in recognition. I returned the nod, and went back to my drawing.

I knew that she was an addict, but mentally I separated drug counselors into a small annoying subgroup apart from the rest of us. They were the professional addicts; they made a living at it. She seemed out of place in a room full of amateurs. I was also uneasy because she knew so much about me. She'd been there when I was going through the shakes and learning to eat again. She'd heard my lifeline. She'd been the butt of the golf protest, the pointless rebellion, and my last attempt to hold on to my addictions. I didn't want her to be at Murdock's.

After the meeting I spoke to her, but she didn't remember my name. I vividly remembered Tess, but to her I was just one of the endless stream of alkies that she dealt with in order to collect a paycheck at the end of the month. Her presence at Murdock's was part of her own personal struggle. It had nothing to do with me.

I wanted to apologize to her about the golf club. The memory of it was a symbol of the time when I believed that sarcasm was creative, that glossing the damage I did with humor made it all right. But if she didn't remember me she was unlikely to have given much importance to the exercise of group petulance I had helped organize on the Manor lawn. Tess did, however, remember Wayne. My old counselor had given up the counseling business to become an assistant coach for Portland's minor league hockey team. I vowed to look him up. I wanted him to know I was still sober. I wanted him to be proud of me.

Within a few days of seeing Tess I ran into Stevie. I had just come from the library and spotted her reading the newspaper at a table in front of one of those espresso shops that had sprung up every few feet on Portland streets. I walked up behind her and said, "Hey rube, what brings you to the big city?"

"Oh shit," she said, "how are you?" Her smile was genuine and we embraced for a moment. "Sit down," she ordered. For a while the two of us just stared at each other. She looked good.

"So how goes it?" I asked.

"Great," she said. "I'm being a housewife and I love it. I'm doing home schooling with my kids. I relearn things in the afternoon and try to teach the stuff to them the next morning."

"No more real estate?" I asked.

"No. People will just have to live where they're at from now on. How's Isol?"

"She's doing fine. I'm working. I do store inventories and stay out of jail."

"That's always good," she said. "What about the Bar?"

"I've applied. I expect to hear from them any day." The big question hung in the air between us. We sipped our coffee and stared at each other. She looked healthy and vibrant. I didn't want to ruin the moment, but it had to be asked. "Have you stayed clean?"

"Yes," she said, "and you?"

"AA, all the way?"

"Oh, thank God." She grabbed my hand. "We're the one in ten that makes it. I didn't think I'd be the one. I didn't think you were either."

"How did you do it?"

"I'm not sure," she said. "At first I think it was stubbornness. I saw it as me against the addiction and I wasn't going to lose. You know how it goes, 'I want what I want and I want it now.' Well, I wanted sobriety and I was going to hold my breath until I got it, but in the end I couldn't do it with stubbornness. When I ran out of breath, I just gave up. When I did, the craving was gone, or at least, it was hardly there. I'm an addict. I know that. I'll always be an addict. I don't care. I even like being an addict. But I don't use."

"So is the urge really gone?" I asked.

"More or less," she said. "It crosses my mind. Driving by a hospital still gives me the kind of back pain that can only be cured by a virile young intern with a bottle of Percodan, but I just drive on by."

"Does it have to be a virile young intern?" I asked.

"Absolutely," she said. "How about you? How'd you do it?"

"I got God," I said.

"You're shittin' me," Stevie said, almost knocking over her coffee. "You got God?"

"Yep," I said, "came to me on a bus."

"I can't believe it," she said. "You are the last person on earth . . . . So do you go to church and everything?"

"Not yet, but I might." I explained about the bus and the Bible and William James and Murdock's.

"So did God take away the urge?" she asked.

"No," I said. "The urge comes back once in a while. Oddly, the places that attract me are the dark dirty alkie bars that open at six in the morning so the regulars can drink away the shakes. They are anonymous doors to the other world."

"Does God keep you out of those places?"

"Maybe," I said. "Maybe he gives me the strength to stay out. I haven't gone in yet."

"Are you going to practice law?"

"I don't know. Right now I just want the choice back. Now, I can choose whether I want to drink or not. I'd lost that choice. If I get admitted I'll choose whether I want to practice or not."

"Well, if you go back, call me. I'll have you write me a will or something."

"You got it," I told her. "What do you hear from our comrades at the Manor?"

"Not much," she said. "Everyone went his or her own way. You went to Murdock's. I have a group in my house. Most everybody else just went out again."

"Have you heard from Daniel?" I asked.

"Yeah," she said, "he went out about a month ago."

"Damn," I said. "Booze or coke?"

"Both."

I stewed for a couple of days about Daniel and then I called. I pretended that I didn't know. After the normal preliminaries about what we had been doing, I asked.

"I went out," he said.

"That's what Stevie said."

"I knew she couldn't keep quiet about it."

"Hey," I said, "it's us. No secrets. Are you still using?"

"I did last weekend."

"How is it?"

"It's the same as it was."

"Do you get high?"

"Yeah."

"So why did you do it?"

"I don't really know. It was what I wanted to do. It's what I do. Sobriety was not kind to me. It was an interminable emptiness. It was going to work and coming home, trudging a road that wasn't mine for reasons I didn't understand. I went to AA and NA, hell I went to all the A's, but I never really settled into anything. I never joined a group and none of them offered to take me in. Maybe that was a mistake. I hung around the program, I watched it at work in people, but

I never really got it. The craving never went away."

"Are you going to try again?"

"I'm thinking I need to find a group and become part of it. You've done that. You go to Murdock's. Is that why it worked for you?"

"Not really," I said. "I had an experience, a God experience."

"You had it, the real thing?"

"It was the real thing."

"That's terribly unfair," he said. "That's what I want. That's all I want, and I don't get it. When was yours?" I told him the same story I told to Stevie.

"You're enlightened," he said afterward.

"I suppose," I answered. "A little bit."

"Can you make it happen for me?" he asked.

"No." Our conversation came to an end.

"I'll see you at Murdock's," he said, but I never saw him there.

I didn't feel bad about Daniel. He had his own road to follow, and for the time being addiction was part of it. I had a sense that I will always be attracted to addicts. In Old Town—Portland's narcotics market-place—the alkies, addicts, and mentally ill loiter on street corners and sleep in doorways. They frighten the normies away from the Old Town businesses. Theirs is a harsh and violent world driven by the next bottle of Mad Dog or the next needle full of black tar heroin. They speak a different language and dress in the fashions of the street. To normies, they are a social problem, a phenomenon to be discussed at city counsel meetings. To me, they are family. I know that I am always welcome there. They have a home for me, a street corner, a tavern, and a doorstep waiting for the day I come home. I am the prodigal son. They are ready to celebrate my return and for that I will always love them.

Talking to Daniel reminded me what a lonely journey I was on. My home was with the people who closed out their days in bars, the cops drinking away the stress of the last shift, the school teachers like Daniel snorting cocaine in tavern bathrooms to escape the tediousness of public education. My people drank and used. Because I didn't, they no longer wanted me around them.

I was now also apart from the normal world where people went about life pursuing careers and rearing children as if those were natural things to do. They had company picnics, family reunions, and church on Sunday. I had Murdock's and a God that I'd compared to a hamster.

The Bar finally responded to all the papers I'd sent them. The Oregon Supreme Court had decided that I should be on probation for three years. During that time I was to abstain from alcohol and drugs and attend at least one AA meeting per week. I was assigned a probation officer to make quarterly reports about my compliance.

The pointlessness of my probation seemed to emphasize the gap between our two worlds. Throughout the reinstatement process the bar had been represented by a very kind woman who had advocated my reinstatement. I tried to explain to her the sadness of it all. "You see," I told her, "if I stay clean and attend AA meetings I will report that I am clean and attending meetings. If I go out and start using again, I will report that I am clean and attending meetings. Drugs and lies go together. A urine test would be more practical." She seemed to understand, but the idea of a urine test was entirely too distasteful for the Bar. They chose to believe in integrity.

My probation officer, an alcoholic lawyer who'd been sober for twenty years, had no problem seeing the humor of it. He knew that no one had ever stopped using because of probation. Judges who sentence people to AA do a disservice to the convict and to AA. The Bar had made the same mistake. My new probation officer assured me that he would make the positive reports about me as long as he had a scintilla of belief they were true. I received a new Bar card, and was once again an attorney.

My probation officer was the titular head of a group of lawyers and doctors in recovery. They met every Thursday evening, and at my probation officer's suggestion, I began to attend. For the first couple of meetings I felt awkward and out of place. I didn't feel like a lawyer. The people at the meetings came from offices wearing suits and ties, the accoutrements of their careers. They looked like lawyers, but they drank like I did. It was a group for drunks. Some of the members were prominent in legal and political circles. Others were more like me, struggling to regain lost licenses or restart careers that had drowned in alcohol. I came to enjoy the meetings, but Murdock's was my home.

I called my parents to tell them about being readmitted to the Bar. I had not been a particularly good son and our conversations were never satisfying on either side. However, I thought they would be pleased that in a technical sense I was a lawyer again.

"When do you think you'll start practicing?" my father asked.

"I don't know," I said. He liked the idea of my being a lawyer. He gave me a pep talk about setting goals and being able to accomplish anything if I set my mind to it. I couldn't explain to him that I no longer trusted my mind. He talked of goals, empowerment, and persistence. For him, success was a real place, and with a little effort anyone, even a reformed drunk, could get there. He was trying to be helpful but only managed to make me sad. I wasn't competent to set goals. Being empowered seemed the way to do more damage.

My mother was more concerned about where I was than where I was going. "I admire your will power for being able to stay away from the drugs," she told me. She always liked to emphasize the drugs, as if they were qualitatively different from alcohol. "It must be a day to day battle." To her sobriety was about curbing the urge to drink. For me it was restructuring the things I believed and the way I thought. Since leaving the Manor I'd had only a few flashes of the craving, and they had gone away easily. God had not taken away my desire to drink. Instead he had moved into the place where it used to live. I didn't understand the second consciousness living in my head, but I understood intuitively that alcohol would drive it away. It had taken far too many years to find him to lose him for the sake of one last drunk. I didn't talk about God to my mother. She figured I was crazy enough as it was.

The conversation with my mother made me feel lonely again. One of my first feelings at the Manor was that straight people couldn't help me; if I was ever to stay sober I would have to look to other addicts. Outside the Manor that feeling translated into a sense that there would always be an impenetrable wall of misunderstanding between the normies and me. I would never know what it is like to be straight. I would never think the way straight people think. I was apart from using addicts as well. Alcoholics who don't drink are not welcome where the users gather. Neither the customers nor the proprietors of taverns want a recovering alcoholic on the premises. The mere presence of such a person steals the taste from the beer. In AA, there is the belief that we choose and embrace anonymity. In living, however, it is more often forced upon us.

No one was anonymous at Murdock's. Attendance there remained as regular for me as my attendance had once been at Taps. In certain respects Murdock's was much the same as the taverns. The regulars assembled at predictable times, told predictable stories, and bickered among themselves. Newcomers, and those just passing through town, showed up for a while and then disappeared. It was a place to relax and be who I was. Stepping into Murdock's was like putting on comfortable shoes and being home again.

Isol came to accept my trips to Murdock's as a necessary part of my life. I was a calmer and nicer person when I returned from AA meetings. She liked that.

Isol was an enigma to me. She had just stopped using. I didn't bring it up much, but when we were using she had downed the liquor, smoked marijuana, and snorted cocaine in the same proportion to her body weight as had I. Seeing her passed out on the living room floor had been as regular an occurrence as our trips to Taps. I considered it possible that she was simply a heavy drinker, the kind who enjoys a good drunk but can stop for any reason or no reason whenever the desire to do so appeared. Heavy drinking does not make a normal person alcoholic, just as sobriety does not make an alcoholic normal. Another possibility was that she was an alkie, but she had stopped by sheer force of will. If this were the case she was suffering. She could be sober, but not at ease.

In the evenings as we read or watched television I often pondered her situation. It was not my job to pronounce other people alcoholic, but our proximity and our newly blossoming marriage made it something for me to consider. It seemed to me that she didn't care to hear about what happened at Murdock's. This made me think she was one of us. Normies are curious about what goes on at AA, in the same way that non-members are curious about what happens behind the closed doors of an Elks Club. Alcoholics, on the other hand, find any mention of AA in poor taste. For serious drinkers, AA is not nearly anonymous enough. I could not tell whether Isol's disinterest in Murdock's was out of boredom or fear.

I eventually stopped trying to diagnose Isol. The concept that we were simply different settled comfortably on me. Diagnosing other people is an exercise designed to find something wrong. Finding defects in people had ceased to give me the satisfaction it once did, so to the extent possible, I quit. Within reason, I could let each person have his or her own sobriety. I didn't have to meddle.

Winter rains had come again to Oregon. Christmas arrived and there were presents beneath the tree. Isol and I opened them without hangovers and felt that for the first time in years we truly had something for which to be thankful.

One Saturday in February I was donning my coat to venture into the rain for the noon meeting at Murdock's when I asked Isol if she'd like to come along. I'd asked her many times before, both because I thought she might need what was there and so she wouldn't feel that it was a secret place from which she was excluded. Her answer had always been a polite thanks, but no thanks. On this particular rainy day she said okay.

As we walked there I explained to her how the meeting worked—how people shared when called upon, that no one was permitted to comment upon what another person said, and that she might hear a lot about God. I told her she'd probably be called on to speak and that, if she was uneasy about it, she could simply pass.

The crowd at Murdock's was a predictable collection of old timers, lunch time drop-ins, and recent treatment center graduates. She and I took seats at a my regular table in front of the chairman's desk. People expected me to be there. This time Isol was with me.

The meeting proceeded as meetings had proceeded there for twenty years. The Twelve Steps and the Twelve Traditions were read aloud. When newcomers were welcomed, Isol raised her hand to signify that it was her first AA meeting ever. The chairman then read from the Big Book and began calling on people to speak.

As the speakers shared, I lapsed into the zone of comfort that always came over me in meetings. Each person who spoke was a reminder of where I'd been and an affirmation of what I had today. That feeling of comfort was my substitute for drugs. In it I had found what I had always looked for in the bottle. My God could rest when I was in the meeting. For ninety minutes I would be tended by others.

Kentucky Ken had shared. Big Amos had told some of his story. Arlene was speaking when I came out of my reverie and looked at Isol. Tears were streaming down her face. She was hearing her own story being told by another. The veil of loneliness was being pulled aside. She was seeing that she was not alone. She was one of us. She was coming home.

About the Author

Orrin Onken is a probate lawyer who practices in Fairview, Oregon.